D1462474

THE SEA ROVERS

Pirates, Privateers,
and Buccaneers

THE SEA ROVERS

Pirates, Privateers, and Buccaneers

by ALBERT MARRIN

Illustrated with old prints and engravings,
diagrams and maps.

Atheneum 1984 New York

LIBRARY OF CONGRESS CATALOGING IN PUBLICATION DATA

Marrin, Albert.   The sea rovers.

SUMMARY: Discusses Drake, Morgan, Blackbeard, and
other pirates and privateers, both men and women, who
have roamed the sea since 1500.
1. Pirates—Juvenile literature.   [1. Pirates]
I. Title.
G535.M33   1984   364.1′64 [920]   83-15886
ISBN 0-689-31029-3

Published simultaneously in Canada by
McClelland & Stewart, Ltd.
Composition by Maryland Linotype, Baltimore, Maryland
Printed and bound by Fairfield Graphics,
Fairfield, Pennsylvania
Designed by Marilyn Marcus
First Edition

A bolder race of men, both as to personal valor and conduct, certainly never yet appeared on the liquid element or dry land.

—John Esquemeling,
The Buccaneers of America,
1684

Contents

	Foreword	ix
I	*Drake the Sea King*	3
II	*The Rise of the Buccaneers*	35
III	*Henry Morgan, The Buccaneer Prince*	59
IV	*The Golden Age of Piracy*	87
V	*The Devil's Twins:* *Captain Kidd and Blackbeard*	108
VI	*Sisters in Crime:* *Women under the Jolly Roger*	128
VII	*The Barbary Pirates and* *the United States Navy*	141
	Some More Books	169
	Index	171

Foreword

This is the story of that adventurous breed of men (and sometimes women) who roamed the seas in search of other people's wealth. It is not a new story; in fact it is one of the oldest stories in the world. Seafaring and sea roving were born at the same time. Ever since people learned to sail in ships, others have made their living by robbing them.

Sea rovers have nearly changed the course of history more than once. A young Roman nobleman fell into the hands of Mediterranean pirates about the year 79 B.C. They treated him kindly, hoping to gain a large ransom for such an important person. The ransom was paid, but before leaving, the young man promised, smiling all the while, that he'd return to repay the insult. Julius Caesar did return, with a Roman fleet, and had every pirate crucified.

Great nations have been founded by sea rovers. The Vikings settled Norway, Sweden, and Denmark. *Viking* means "pirate" in the ancient Norse language. These fierce warrior-sailors terrorized Europe during the early Middle Ages (600–1000 A.D.), massacring people, burning towns, and looting churches. They came in long, dragon-headed boats powered by sails and oars. The oarsmen, called *Rus*, ventured deep into the land that borrowed their name: Russia, Land of the Pirate Oarsmen.

Not all sea rovers were pirates—outlaws. As we shall see, privateers and buccaneers, although they lived by stealing, had the law on their side.

Our story is about the "golden age" of sea roving that began when Columbus discovered the New World and lasted for three hundred years. The action centers at first in the Caribbean Sea, along the mainland of South America and the islands that stretch in a huge arc southward from Florida to Venezuela. Eventually the action became worldwide, as sea rovers left the Caribbean to plunder the coasts of North America, Africa, India, and the lands bordering the Red Sea. The Barbary states of North Africa are examples of entire countries that lived by piracy.

Countless thousands have gone sea roving since the 1500s. We shall never know the names of any but a few of these; they did not leave business cards. Of those we do know, most were small-time thieves happy to attack, kill, and run away with their loot. A *very few* were unusual people who left their mark on history. Who they were, what they did, and how they did it always has, and always will, capture our imaginations.

Albert Marrin
New York City

THE SEA ROVERS

Pirates, Privateers, and Buccaneers

I

Drake the Sea King

The harbor, Plymouth, England, October 2, 1567. It is a bright autumn morning with a gusty breeze blowing from the land.

The young man on the ship's bridge holds his breath for a long moment, then releases it slowly. His heart pounds with excitement.

On the flagship nearby, trumpeters raise their instruments, sending hard, metallic notes echoing across the harbor. Instantly, barefooted sailors clad in gaily colored canvas jackets and trousers rush to their posts. Some strain at the bars of heavy wooden wheels, making ropes creak against wood as anchors rise dripping and muddy from the harbor bottom. Others scurry up rope ladders to the yardarms, the cross-pieces on the masts from which the sails hang. There is a rustle of loose canvas and suddenly the sails blossom as they catch the breeze.

Slowly, silently, the wind breathes life into the wooden hulls. They move, dipping and rolling and tossing white spray as they gain speed. From the shore comes the boom and clang of cannon and churchbells bidding the seamen Godspeed.

Six ships, one behind the other, glide out of the harbor, heading for open water. Five minutes. Fifteen minutes. A half-hour. No sound comes from the land anymore.

There is different music now; the whistling of the wind in the shrouds* and the slap, slap, slapping of low waves against the bows.

The young man relaxes. At last he, Francis Drake, is sailing toward his first real adventure. He had worked hard and sacrificed much for this day. Born in 1545, Drake at twenty-two was short, broad-shouldered, with the muscular limbs of an athlete. Already his skin was weatherbeaten and leathery.

His whole life had been spent near salt water or upon it. The Drakes had always been sea people. Edmund Drake, the father, supported his wife and twelve children by Bible-reading and preaching aboard ships when they came into port. It was a poorly-paid occupation, and for several years the family could only afford to live on a mastless, rotten hulk anchored offshore. Francis's earliest memories were of skipping flat stones across the water and of being rocked to sleep by the gentle rising and falling of his home as it rode the tides.

Francis learned as a boy to look to the sea for his living. As the eldest child, he had to go to work soonest. At about the age of ten, his father found him a job on a tiny vessel that traded between England and Holland. His schoolroom was no ordinary place of desks and books, but the North Sea, with its howling winds and mud-thick fogs. He had no choice: either he became a good pupil or followed count-less others to a watery grave. He learned to navigate by the stars, to steer clear of rocky coastlines, to go without sleep during storms when waves towered over the ship's mast. His employer, a childless bachelor, became fond of the youngster and remembered him in his will. And so, at six-teen, Francis Drake was able to buy a ship and become its skipper.

Voyage followed voyage, and at the end of each there were always some coins to put aside after paying expenses.

---

* Shrouds are ropes leading from the tops of the masts to the sides of the ship to keep the masts steady.

Francis Drake in later life. Drake was so successful in his raids against the Spaniards that they thought the Devil was helping him locate their ships with a magical crystal ball he kept in his ship's cabin.

Drake scrimped and saved, finally selling his boat to invest in a scheme that promised to make him rich. That scheme was the idea of his cousin, John Hawkins, who, at thirty-five, had a genius for turning dreams into gold. Everything depended upon the little fleet he led out of Plymouth that fine morning. Hawkins's flagship was the *Jesus*, a seven hundred-tonner mounting twenty-five cannon; she, together with *Minion*, a three hundred-tonner, belonged to Queen Elizabeth. "Good Queen Bess" was also "Clever Queen Bess," because she gladly lent Royal Navy ships for

schemes that promised high profits. The other vessels—
William and John, Swallow, Angel, Judith—were much
smaller and lightly armed. Drake commanded the fifty-ton
Judith.

The maps called their destination Guinea, West Africa.
But the sailors knew it by another name: The Slave Coast.
For the cousins and their Queen were traders in Negro
slaves. Hawkins's plan was to capture slaves, ship them to

*Hawkins's little fleet was nearly destroyed by the Spaniards at
San Jose de Ulua. Later, Hawkins was knighted by Queen
Elizabeth for his service in the Battle of the Spanish Armada.*

the New World, and sell them to the Spanish settlers there at a huge profit. This sounds to us like a cruel, dirty business. Yet we must remember that the sea rovers were people of their age, as we are of ours. And in their age the idea that some people should own others and live off their labors seemed natural. Being a slave trader did not make one less of a "gentleman" in the eyes of his countrymen.

Drake's *Judith* and her companions sailed steadily southward. Africa was still the "Dark Continent," a mysterious land, to Europeans. Drake had heard of its strange creatures and probably believed in some of them. There were oyster trees and seahorses that kicked ships apart. You had to be especially careful near the weeping crocodiles; they cried so sadly that, feeling sorry for them, you came too close—then they bit you in half.

Drake saw no marvelous beasts this time. Nor did he see many people, because the Africans knew what the strangers wanted and hid whenever they appeared. Only by joining in a tribal war were they able to capture about five hundred people from the losing side. Its slave decks full, in February, 1568, the fleet set course toward the setting sun.

At least seven weeks of sailing separated the Old World from the New; seven weeks of loneliness on the wide, watery desert of the Atlantic Ocean. Drake knew that once Africa faded into the distance they would see no other people until they arrived on the western shore. It felt as if they were the only people in the world.

Everyone, including the slaves, was eager for the sight of land after such a journey. The lookouts high in the crows' nests scanned the horizon with growing eagerness, for whoever made the first sighting could claim a gold chain as his reward. Land had to be near, as the color of the water was changing from the dark blue of mid-ocean to the green of offshore shallows. Sea gulls appeared, and chunks of driftwood. Sailors hauled in a twisted branch and found it crawling with inch-long carpenter ants.

"Land ho!" "Land ho!"

The English had come too far to waste time. The Caribbean Sea, that immense arm of the Atlantic, was their highway to wealth. After taking on fresh water, they began to visit the settlements along the Spanish Main, the mainland of South America stretching along the coast from Venezuela to Panama.

Hawkins had to be careful, for his fleet was trespassing in these waters. Ever since 1494, the Spaniards had claimed the whole New World for themselves. Since their explorer, Christopher Columbus, had discovered it, they claimed it was theirs to do with as they pleased. And it pleased them to keep out foreigners; indeed, not even a Spanish merchant could sail there on his own. Every ship bound for America had to join a convoy that sailed from Spain twice a year and was protected by warships. All trade goods had to be Spanish-made or have a Spanish license and pay taxes to the Spanish government. Since there were never enough people to work the mines and plantations, slaves were the most valuable and the most heavily taxed "trade goods."

The Spanish government became its own enemy and the smugglers' friend. Spanish settlers hated to pay taxes on things they needed. They were eager to trade with the English, who sold cheaply and tax-free, as long as they weren't caught.

Hawkins solved their problem. Upon arriving at a coastal town, he sent a messenger ashore with a letter to the mayor. Politely he explained that a storm had blown him off course and that he wanted to sell slaves in order to buy fresh supplies. The mayor, of course, did his duty: he called the English outlaws and threatened to fight if they didn't go away at once. This was exactly what Hawkins expected him to say. Immediately the ugly snouts of *Jesus*'s and *Minion*'s cannon were pointed toward the town. Armed landing parties rowed ashore to back up Hawkins's "request" to trade.

Drums beat. Flags waved. Guns blazed.

It was all very exciting, although no one was hurt; no one was *supposed* to be hurt. Hawkins had only put on an act to allow the settlers to tell their government that they had been forced to buy the things they needed at gunpoint. Hawkins then gave them letters praising their courage in resisting him.

Everyone was happy with this arrangement—everyone except the tax collectors. Hawkins did a "brisk trade," adding another bag of gold coins to the strongbox in his cabin after each stop along the coast. By September, 1568, most of the slaves were sold and he set a course for Plymouth. Cousin Francis, now a rich man, was glad.

Yet he counted his riches too soon. As the fleet rounded the western tip of Cuba, it ran into a hurricane. These Caribbean storms made those of the North Sea seem like gentle spring showers. The wind whooped at one hundred miles an hour. Flowers from ashore, even small lizards, were carried far out to sea by the wind gusts. The storm nearly sank the *Jesus*, although doing less damage to her sister ships.

One gray morning a few days later a line of ships sailed into the harbor of San Juan de Ulua, a low-lying island near Vera Cruz, the chief port of New Spain (Mexico). The townspeople had been expecting a special guest and cheered as the ships swept up to the seawall and dropped anchor. But their cheers stuck in their throats as the English swarmed ashore. Hawkins explained that he meant no harm. He had come because he needed a sheltered harbor in which to repair his ships and would pay for any supplies he took.

The Englishmen set to work, replacing broken timbers and patching torn sails. Repairs were going along well until, a few days later, *Jesus*'s lookouts noticed something strange. They rubbed their eyes in disbelief, looked again, and shouted "Sails ho!" On the horizon, moving fast, they counted one, two . . . thirteen ships advancing under full sail.

Their visitors were not ordinary vessels, but royal ships on a mission from Spain's King Philip II. Not only did they outnumber the English, they outgunned them as

La Verra Crvs

An early Spanish drawing of Vera Cruz, chief port of Mexico. Off the mainland can be seen the low-lying island of San Juan de Ulua with its seawall running the length of the harbor. Here is where John Hawkins suffered the worst defeat of his career, and where Francis Drake vowed revenge against the Spaniards.

well, for two of the ships were galleons, the battleships of the 1500s. Each galleon carried five hundred soldiers and sailors, plus dozens of cannon. In command was Don Martin Enriquez, the governor of New Spain. San Juan de Ulua's special guest had arrived.

What should Hawkins do? He gladly would have sailed away before Don Martin came near, but *Jesus*'s masts were still being repaired. He could have kept the Spaniards out of the harbor, for his men controlled the guns along the seawall and could blow them to bits if they entered. But that would have been an act of war and therefore treason. Queen Elizabeth alone could declare war, and she was still at peace with Spain.

Both commanders decided to talk rather than fight. After some hard bargaining they agreed that the Spaniards could enter the harbor as long as they kept their distance and the English kept control of the seawall guns. Don Martin gave his word as a gentleman that the English could complete their repairs and leave in peace.

Too bad his promise was worthless. Don Martin knew all about *"Achines de Plimua"*—Hawkins of Plymouth—the rascal who broke his king's laws. He saw Hawkins as a criminal with whom a nobleman need not play fair. No sooner was the agreement signed than he called his captains together and ordered them to make plans to break it. Once the English let down their guard, he would wipe them out.

Yet John Hawkins was not an easy man to trick. Things just didn't *feel* right. The Spaniards were too polite, too quick to smile. At night he heard unexplained movements between their ships, saw too many glimmerings of moonlight reflecting off steel helmets. Maybe Don Martin could be trusted, maybe not. Better to hope for the best while preparing for the worst.

Hawkins doubled his lookouts and readied his ships for battle. Officers put on steel helmets and breastplates decorated with elaborate designs. Weapons rooms were opened and swords, muskets, bows and arrows placed within easy reach along the decks. Sailors formed human chains to pass gunpowder bags and cannon balls from hand to hand, stacking them in neat piles beside the guns. Cabin boys sprinkled sand on the decks to prevent them becoming slippery with blood. Now they were ready, and waiting.

Don Martin didn't keep them waiting long. Two days later, September 23, 1568, a trumpet sounded from his flagship. Instantly hundreds of Spanish soldiers jumped from their ships onto the island. Shots rang out, swords flashed, and within a few minutes every Englishman guarding the seawall guns was dead. Their sacrifice bought precious seconds for their brothers aboard the ships. At the first shots the English sailors grabbed axes and long oars called "sweeps." As some cut the ropes that held the ships to the seawall, others pushed against it with their sweeps.

Seconds passed like hours as *Jesus* and *Minion* began to drift from shore. They drifted maybe thirty yards when the nearest enemy vessels, the galleons, came in range. The English opened fire first.

It was terrible, though also strangely wonderful, to see the guns go into action. Each gun captain held a "match," a slow-burning rope attached to a forked stick called a linstock. The moment he put the match to the touchhole at the rear of the cannon, it set off the gunpowder charge in the barrel.

BAR-O-O-O-M.

The cannon became a roaring, kicking, flame-spitting monster. Its blast set the gunners' ears ringing. If they were not fast enough, its kickback might snap their legs like dry twigs.

The gunners lost track of time once they took up the rhythm of their work. Each gun became a living being and they existed only to push "food" down its open mouth.

Load. Ram a bag of gunpowder down the cannon's muzzle. Next roll down a sixteen-pound iron ball followed by old rags packed in for a tight fit.

Aim.

Fire.

Jump clear.

Clean the barrel with a damp sheepskin mop and start all over again.

The deck filled with clouds of choking, stinging black smoke. The men, shirtless and sweating, turned black themselves as gunpowder particles stuck to their damp bodies. They stank like cattle, although everyone was too busy to notice.

The English gunners fired often and well. Their first shots slammed into a galleon. An explosion rocked the great ship and it disappeared in a ball of orange flame. Another volley burst through the timbers of Don Martin's galleon at the waterline. Sailors screamed, or simply died

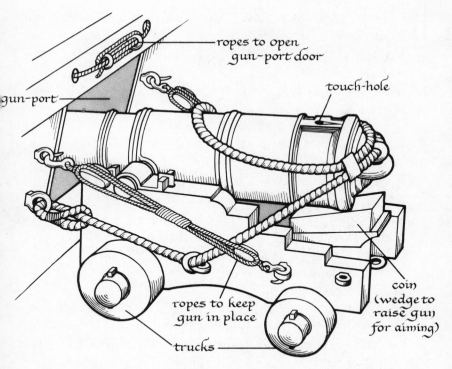

ropes to open
gun-port door

touch-hole

gun-port

coin
(wedge to
raise gun
for aiming)

ropes to keep
gun in place

trucks

A HEAVY SAILING-SHIP CANNON. *Such weapons could hurl an iron ball weighing as much as sixty-eight pounds over half a mile. A fast crew could clean, load, and fire the cannon every three or four minutes.*

without making a sound, cut down by wooden splinters that whizzed about like razor blades; splinters always killed more men than direct hits by cannon balls. The survivors abandoned ship as the harbor water washed over the main deck.

The real duel, however, was between the ships and the shore batteries, and here everything favored the Spaniards. Even as the galleons burned, Hawkins knew he had lost the battle. Once the enemy recaptured these cannon, they were able to turn them against his ships. The guns were so close and so well-placed that a blind person couldn't miss.

At pointblank range the Spaniards sent a hailstorm of iron at *Jesus*, their chief target. Jagged holes pockmarked her hull from waterline to poop, the highest deck at the stern. Repair parties dodged flying splinters to work on the worst damage. Lead sheets were nailed into place at the waterline and shot-plugs hammered in; a shot-plug was a piece of wood shaped like an ice cream cone to fit most holes in a ship's side.

Drake and the others fought as best they could, but Hawkins was the hero of this battle. He was everywhere, giving orders and encouragement. He fought surrounded, it seemed, by an invisible shield that protected him from harm. Growing thirsty, he had a drink brought in a tall silver cup. Lifting it so everyone could see, he saluted the gunners. As soon as he set down the empty cup, a cannon ball whisked it away as he let go. "Have no fear," Hawkins cried, "for God, who has saved me from this shot, will save us from these villains."

And saved they were, but not before paying an awful price. Only *Minion* and *Judith* survived to limp home across the Atlantic. Left behind were *Jesus* and the others, burned to the water or captured. Gone also were the profits from slaves, and several hundred Englishmen, dead or prisoners.

———◆◆———

"Never forget; never forgive; get even," could have been Francis Drake's motto after San Juan de Ulua. Everything he had worked for since a teenager had been destroyed by Spanish treachery. Because they had wronged him, he felt that everything he did to Spaniards from now on was right. He vowed to pay them back with interest many, many times over. He began by capturing the treasure house of the whole Spanish Main.

That treasure house was located on the Isthmus of Panama. An isthmus is a narrow strip of land, bordered on both sides by water, joining two larger bodies of land. The Isthmus of Panama is bordered by the Caribbean sea on the east and the Pacific Ocean on the west; it joins South and Central America. Across its waist traveled most of the riches of the New World.

To understand Drake's plan, we should imagine Panama City on the Pacific coast as the mouth of a giant funnel. Treasure poured into this mouth from all sides. From the mines of Central America came ships bearing chests of gold. From the offshore islands—The Pearl Islands —came thousands of gray-blue pearls. From Peru came ships that rode low in the water, weighed down with sacks of green emeralds and tons of silver bars.

The treasure was gathered in Panama City and sent twice a year by mule train through the "neck" of the funnel, a secret jungle trail that ended at Nombre de Dios on the Caribbean side of the Isthmus. There, in the town called "Name of God," the treasure was stored in the king's treasure house to await the fleet that would take it to Spain. Drake intended to loot that treasure house when it was packed to the ceiling with the wealth of the Americas.

Drake was a daring man, but not a foolish one. He realized that the more dangerous the plan, the more carefully it had to be thought out. He made two secret voyages to the Spanish Main (1569, 1571) to study Nombre de Dios and how it might be attacked. He may even have entered the town disguised as a Spanish seaman. On the second voyage he found a small harbor down the coast hidden by the surrounding jungle. He named it Port Pheasant, because the jungle was full of the brightly colored birds. Here was the perfect hideout when the time came to carry out the plan.

In May 1572, Drake slipped quietly out of Plymouth harbor with two small ships, the seventy-ton *Pasha* and the thirty-ton *Swan*. On board were seventy-three men, including Drake's brothers John and Joseph. Only one man was above the age of thirty; they had to be young to face the hardships that lay ahead. *Pasha* also carried three pinnaces made in sections that could easily be fitted together. A pinnace was a small boat powered by sails or sweeps. Being lightweight, it was fast and could escape larger vessels by going into shallow water.

Where did Drake get the money to hire ships and

sailors? We don't know. Probably wealthy people who didn't want their names mentioned paid for the voyage in return for a share of the profits. A good bet is that Queen Elizabeth was part of the group; *Jesus* had been her ship, and she didn't like having her property shot to pieces.

Drake arrived at Port Pheasant on July 12 and began preparing for the raid. Tall trees were chopped down and used to build a fort. Carpenters assembled the pinnaces and camouflaged them with branches. When all was ready, Drake told his men about the plan. Like a modern commando operation, everything depended upon surprise and split-second timing. They would approach Nombre de Dios at dawn, when people least expected trouble. Once ashore, they would overpower the guards, seize the king's treasure house, and escape before the Spaniards realized what happened. But if their timing was off, or something really went wrong, they'd be in big trouble, for several hundred of King Philip's finest troops were stationed in the town.

The pinnaces set out before nightfall on July 28. Gliding silently over the calm sea, they hugged the coastline to avoid enemy ships. Night came, a starless night with storm clouds gathering in the black, velvety sky. Two miles outside the harbor, they dropped anchor and waited for the dawn.

Drake ordered half the men to sleep while the others kept watch. Still, no one aboard the bobbing boats could sleep. These were young men, and inexperienced; most had never been in battle before. Nombre de Dios was no sleepy colonial village, but one of the largest towns in the New World. "It's as big as Plymouth," they whispered, counting the house lights. Fear spread among them like an infection.

The hours ticked by slowly, ever so slowly. Midnight. One by one the lights went out and the town slept. Only the sound of the booming surf came from the shore.

Drake knew that he had to act quickly, before his men's courage disappeared altogether. Just then a great light shone on the water, pointing like a silvery finger

Nombre de Dios (Name of God), the town in which Drake tried and failed to seize a whole year's treasure from South America, is shown in a Spanish drawing of the early 1600s.

straight at Nombre de Dios. The moon had peered out from behind the clouds.

"It is dawn!" Drake cried, knowing full well that he was lying. "Let us set out!" Without thinking, his men began to row toward the town outlined in the distance. The strain of rowing released tension and took their minds off their fear.

The moment they entered the harbor they noticed a tall ship riding at anchor. Suddenly a rowboat shot out from its side, heading for the shore. They had been seen by the ship's crew.

Spaniards and Englishmen rowed for their lives; the one to give the alarm, the other to head them off. The distance between the boats closed rapidly until the Spaniards saw who they were up against. The moonlight made these fellows with swords and muskets look like wild men. The Spaniards broke off the race, heading for the safety of the open sea.

Drake's men dashed toward the seawall the moment they reached shore. One after another the guns mounted on it were tipped off their carriages onto the sand; their captain had learned a painful lesson from the seawall guns of San Juan de Ulua. A lone guard, meanwhile, saw what happened and ran into town shouting at the top of his voice.

Windows opened. Doors slammed. Pinpricks of light cut the darkness. Bells high in the church steeple set up a harsh clanging. Drums beat. Trumpets blared. The Spanish troops were turning out in their battle gear.

Drake knew that the key to the town was the marketplace, where all the main streets came together. He divided his men into two groups. The smaller group under his brother John was sent to approach the marketplace quietly from the east. Drake himself led the larger group, about fifty men. They didn't try to move quietly or to hide. They rushed down the main street, a drummer and trumpeter playing as loudly as they could while the others carried lighted torches. The idea was to distract the defenders, making them think they faced a much larger force.

The English charged—right into a volley of Spanish musket balls. The trumpeter fell, rolled on the ground, and lay still. His companions paused, fired their weapons, and charged again.

A free-for-all broke out in the darkened marketplace. Men went at each other with swords and muskets swung like clubs. All was confusion·until another burst of gunfire shattered the air, this time from behind the Spaniards. John Drake led his men forward with cries of "Saint George for England," at which the Spaniards dropped their weapons and fled down the darkened side streets.

There was no time to enjoy the victory. With church-bells still clanging overhead, Drake forced a prisoner to lead the way to the governor's house.

The Englishmen burst through the front door and found themselves in a vast room lit by a single flickering candle. The sailors froze in their tracks, their mouths open, not believing their eyes. For there, lined up against a wall, was a pile of silver bars ten feet wide, twelve feet high, and seventy feet long. Each bar represented more than an ordinary seaman could earn in ten years of hard work. And now thousands of bars lay in front of them for the taking.

Drake snapped a command. They had not risked their lives for silver; no, not when the king's treasure house bulged with gold and jewels.

As they hurried to the waterfront, a storm broke, forcing them to take shelter in a shed. The rain came down in sheets, driven by high winds. They were miserable. Not only were they soaked to the skin, but the flints that set off their muskets were wet. Spanish war cries were coming from every direction.

Fear returned. In a few more minutes, Drake knew, his men would panic and run away. "Now that I have brought you to the gate of the world's treasure house," he shouted angrily, "blame nobody but yourselves if you don't take anything home with you."

Drake tried to lead them forward but, after a few steps, fell flat on his face. His men became terrified. Looking down, they saw that the impressions of his feet in the sand were filled with blood and that a stream of blood was flowing from his boot. Ever since the battle in the market-place he had tried to hide a dangerous leg wound. He had already lost enough blood to kill most men, but at last even his strength gave out.

Drake revived, but no amount of ordering and cursing could make the men go forward. He was their captain. They loved him, but also needed him, for no one else in their group had the skill to navigate the Atlantic. In spite of his curses they bound his wound and carried him back to the pinnaces. Before they left, they received one more piece of bad news. John Drake had broken into the king's treasure house, only to find it empty. The royal fleet had sailed with the gold and jewels six weeks earlier.

———— ◆•◆ ————

The future looked grim for young Francis Drake. He had no hope of surprising the Spaniards again at Nombre de Dios. Returning to England empty-handed meant that no one would ever trust him with a ship again. He'd be a nobody.

When he felt the most downhearted, help came from a source he least expected. During the fighting at Nombre de Dios, a Negro slave had escaped from his owner and fled to the beached pinnaces. Diego was his name, and he knew as much as any Spaniard about how their treasure was shipped. There was no need to fight a battle, Diego explained. All Drake had to do was ambush a mule train in the "neck" of the funnel across the Isthmus of Panama.

"Impossible!" Drake said, nodding his head in disagreement. His men were sailors, not jungle fighters. No Englishman could find his way in that unmapped wilderness. They would get lost, wander about aimlessly, and finally starve to death.

Diego knew better. He had friends who were as comfortable in the jungle as Drake was aboard ship—the *Cimarron.* "*Cimarron*" comes from the Spanish for "wild," "untamed," "savage." The Spaniards had learned that, although they enslaved the black African, they could not break his spirit. The desire to be free proved stronger than any punishment or torture. Every year hundreds of slaves, men and women, escaped into the jungle, where they intermarried with the Indians. For fifty years these black people and their children had fought a guerrilla war against their former owners. They moved through the jungle silently, striking, then vanishing without a trace.

Diego introduced Drake to his *Cimarron* friends. Of

course they would show him the way to the gold road. Of course they would help him fight the Spaniards. "But why fight for gold?" they wondered. The shiny yellow metal was too soft to be useful in the jungle; they valued iron for making weapons. Drake must have winced when they told of throwing away whole mule-loads of gold because it seemed worthless. Still, if the English wanted gold, then gold they shall have. All the *Cimarrons* wanted in return was a chance to fight the Spaniard and take his weapons.

Now came the bad news. The rainy season had just begun and the Spaniards would not move treasure along the flooded jungle trail for several months. Drake had no choice but to wait patiently for the rains to stop.

It was a terrible time, that winter of 1572. Drake's brother John was killed when he and a few others foolishly attacked a Spanish ship crowded with musketeers. An epidemic of yellow fever swept through Port Pheasant, claiming the life of Drake's other brother, Joseph. Things became so bad that the *Swan* had to be sunk because there weren't enough men to sail her.

At last the *Cimarrons* reported that the gold road was becoming busy again. On Tuesday, February 3, 1573, Drake set out with eighteen men, all those healthy enough to travel, and thirty *Cimarrons*. This time there would be no slip-ups, he thought.

No Englishmen had ever made such a journey before. They marched in single file, in absolute silence so as not to alert enemy patrols. Butterflies with shiny wings rose in blue clouds from the edge of mud puddles, where they gathered to sip the water through long, tube-like mouthparts. Red, yellow, and green parrots cawed in the treetops. All the while the sun struck them full force. Sweat rolled down the Englishmen's bodies, collecting in puddles in their shoes and making a squishing sound as they walked. The marshes gave off a rotting, sour smell that made it hard to hold down one's food.

Those who had once been slave traders came to admire and respect those who had once been slaves. The jungle held no secrets from these blackskinned warriors. They marched through the tangled underbrush as if it was a broad, well-marked highway. Every pair of crossed twigs on the ground, every bent blade of grass, was a road sign to them. When Drake's men tired, they took their bundles, walking barefoot over ground that would have slashed the white men's feet to ribbons.

From the coast they climbed steadily into the rugged hills that run down the center of Panama like the backbone of some prehistoric lizard. These hills are part of the Cordillera, the mountain ridge that stretches unbroken from Alaska to the tip of South America. As they approached the crest on the fourth day, the *Cimarrons* led Drake to a gigantic old tree with handgrips carved in its side. Climbing to the top, Drake saw the Pacific Ocean stretching before him to the horizon. Then and there he begged God to allow him to be the first Englishman to sail its waters.

A few days later forty-eight men lay hidden in the high grass on either side of a narrow jungle trail near Panama City. Night was falling, and in about an hour three mule trains would be coming down the trail. A *Cimarron* spy had learned that one of these belonged to the Treasurer of Peru, who was returning to Spain with hundreds of pounds of gold dust.

Drake's men were already spending their riches in their imaginations when the sun set. A hush fell over the jungle, broken only by insects' buzzings and the croakings of tree frogs.

The soft tinkling of mules' bells came from the direction of Panama City. Englishmen and *Cimarron* tightened his grip on his weapon and peered out from between the blades of grass. Soon. Soon it would be all over.

Moments later the sound of hoofbeats came from the opposite direction. A Spanish gentleman was riding along the trail at a trot when suddenly he dug his spurs into his horse and sped past the ambush at a gallop. Drake was not worried by this strange behavior, for his men were invisible in the grass.

The mule-bells, meanwhile, grew louder. Drake blew a whistle and his men charged, driving away the guards. Eager hands were forced into mule-packs, only to come out with potatoes instead of gold coins and jewels. Drake learned the truth from a captured guard. One of his men had been drinking brandy to keep up his courage. He became so "brave" that he jumped up, intending to dance a jig on the trail in front of the horseman. A *Cimarron* had knocked him down and covered him with his own body as the rider passed. But it was too late and the rider galloped ahead to warn of the ambush. The Treasurer of Peru simply sent a food train ahead to spring the trap while he returned to Panama City with his treasure. Drake swallowed his anger, saying only that the treasurer must be an honest man, otherwise God would not have allowed him to be saved by a fool. There was nothing left to do now but return to the seacoast and start over again.

Drake's luck changed soon after, when a French ship caught sight of one of the pinnaces. Drake and the French commander, Captain Tetu, agreed to join forces and to share the loot equally. Instead of attacking the mule trains at the beginning of their journey near Panama City, Drake decided to reverse his plan, striking when they neared the end of the line. One evening the *Cimarrons* guided thirty-five Englishmen and Frenchmen to a spot in the jungle outside Nombre de Dios. They camped so close to the town that they could hear the hammerings and sawings of the carpenters working on the galleons in the harbor; repairs were done at night to avoid the scorching daytime heat.

The raiders awoke at dawn to the familiar tinkling of distant mule bells. This time everything went like clockwork. The ambush was well set, and soon the trap closed on one hundred twenty treasure-loaded mules. The Spanish guards were so surprised that they fled after firing only a few shots. Drake's men whooped and danced when they realized that their sufferings had paid off at last. After sharing the loot with the French and saying goodbye to his *Cimarron* friends, Drake set sail for home. Of the seventy-three men who had begun the voyage, forty had died. The survivors, though, could live comfortably for years to come. Diego, who returned with Drake, was fast becoming an Englishman.

On August 9, 1573, Drake's guns roared their greeting and were answered by a thundering salute from Plymouth's shore batteries. It was Sunday morning and most townspeople were in church. The preacher had just begun the sermon when the news came. Within a minute the congregation was on its feet, racing for the harbor below.

◆◆◆

No one today knows how Drake spent the next four years. His backers, having taken their share of the treasure, probably told him to "get lost" until the Spanish ambassador lost interest in the "*pirates*." Drake did as he was told, and it is not until 1577 that we meet him again. Queen Elizabeth had called him to London. Although still at peace, England and Spain were not on friendly terms. As a Protestant country, England feared Spain, Europe's leading Roman Catholic nation. The 1500s were a time of religious strife, when Protestant and Catholic damned each other as "unbelievers" and "enemies of God." The Spanish-ruled Protestant Netherlands had declared its independence. King Philip II sent an army to burn Dutch cities and massacre their citizens. English hearts were with the Dutch, whom they aided with money and weapons. The Spaniards struck back by arresting English merchants and seizing their ships.

Queen Elizabeth wanted revenge, but not open war. Revenge was something Francis Drake knew all about. "Drake," she said, "I would gladly be revenged on the King of Spain for various insults that I have received." Drake bowed deeply and smiled. He already had a plan.

He had never forgotten that day high in the tree overlooking the Pacific Ocean. It would be easy, he thought, to strike the Spaniard where he least expected. No foreigner had ever sailed along the western coast of South America, as there was only one way of entering the Pacific from the East: through the Straits of Magellan, the most dangerous waterway on earth. And so the Spaniards, feeling safe from attack, left their Pacific coast settlements weakly defended and their ships poorly armed. They were as sheep waiting for the wolf.

On November 15, 1577, five ships slipped out of Plymouth harbor unannounced and without fuss. Drake commanded aboard the *Golden Hind*,* a one hundred forty-ton warship armed with thirty long-range cannon and swift as the wind. As commander, Drake occupied the large stern, or rear, cabin. Expensive furniture and carpets made the place feel like a room in the royal palace. He dined like a prince, too, eating off large silver plates while musicians played in the background. The other vessels were the warship *Elizabeth* and three tiny supply ships: *Marigold, Swan, Benedict.*

Only Drake knew the squadron's destination or to whom it belonged. Secrecy was all-important, because Spanish spies kept a close watch on Plymouth. To deceive them, word leaked that the ships were headed for Turkey with trade goods. Yet everything belonged to a secret company in which the Queen was the largest shareholder.

Only when they were far out to sea did Drake reveal their true destination. Some crewmen were happy, seeing this as a chance to get rich. But most grumbled at being tricked into coming along on such a dangerous voyage. What good was a lot of Spanish gold if you weren't alive to spend it? Even one of the officers, Thomas Doughty, began to speak of forcing the captain to return home.

Men were still grumbling when the squadron reached the mouth of the Plate River near present-day Buenos Aires, Argentina. After taking on fresh water, Drake

---

* Originally called the *Pelican*, Drake renamed her *Golden Hind* upon arriving in the New World. We use the more famous name throughout, to avoid confusion.

coasted southward for several hundred miles to a harbor called Port Saint Julian. The port was uninhabited, showing no trace of man except for a rough wooden gallows, the one the Portuguese explorer Ferdinand Magellan had used to hang mutineers fifty-eight years before. The crews immediately understood what Drake had in mind. They were about to go on a dangerous mission whose success depended upon teamwork. There could be only one commander on such a mission; Drake had to assert his authority or they'd be beaten before they began. He had to make an example, and that example was Thomas Doughty.

Drake called the crews together as a jury to hear the case against Doughty. Their verdict: guilty of plotting mutiny. Their sentence: death by beheading. Drake then offered to give a ship to whoever wanted to return to England, warning that if they took the offer and got in his way, he'd blow them out of the water. No one accepted the offer, for no one questioned his authority any longer. After unloading the supplies from *Swan* and *Benedict*, and sinking the empty vessels, Drake set course for the straits of Magellan and the wide waters beyond.

Experienced sailors trembled at the thought of what awaited them. The Straits of Magellan lie between the southernmost tip of South America and a group of offshore islands, Tierra del Fuego—Fireland. Although about three hundred miles long, the straits are often less than a mile wide. The narrow channel is hemmed in by jagged mountains whose peaks lie hidden in clouds and whose sides are covered by glaciers.

The Straits of Magellan seemed jinxed. Sailors believed that witches lurked there, waiting to unleash icy winds and storms against intruders. The sea swarmed, they said, with slithery sea serpents large enough to wind themselves around a ship and swallow it in a gulp.

The English ships struggled against the wind. During calms, the crews landed to fill the water barrels and stock up on fresh meat. They killed thousands of flightless birds, which the Welsh sailors called "whiteheads," or *pen gwynns.* At last, after seventeen days, they left the Straits of Magellan behind.

El Mar Pacifico, "The Peaceful Ocean," is what Magellan had called it. But to Drake it was "The Furious Ocean," or "The Ocean of Sorrows." For no sooner did the English enter the Pacific, than it hit them with the worst storm they had ever seen. For fifty-two days the wind howled and black clouds hid the sun. The ocean boiled and tossed with foam. The ships climbed sixty-foot waves, then dropped suddenly, as if the bottom had fallen out of the earth.

One night men's screams were heard above the storm and *Marigold* disappeared with her whole crew. A few nights later, *Golden Hind* and *Elizabeth* became separated. Thinking Drake lost, *Elizabeth*'s captain sailed back through the Straits of Magellan for home.

At last the storm ended, ending also their bad luck. Although battered and alone, the English were now in the Pacific with a powerful warship. Their arrival caught the Spaniards with their guard down. Sailing northward along the coast of Chile and Peru, *Golden Hind* met many unarmed coastal craft. It was always the same: after boarding, Drake's men took any valuables they found and, equally important, loaded up on fresh food. Drake usually set the ship's crew free, but sometimes kept officers as hostages in case he had to do some hard bargaining later on.

Drake grew bolder with each success. At Callao, the port of Lima, capital of Peru, he gave the Spaniards a show they'd always remember. *Golden Hind* sailed into Callao harbor one morning and dropped anchor. Before the eyes of the people gathered along the waterfront, Drake had himself rowed around the harbor in the longboat. Visiting each Spanish ship in turn, he took its valuables and cut the anchor cables, letting it drift out to sea with the tide. His work done, he calmly raised anchor and sailed away.

Drake also had a surprise at Callao. He learned that the richest treasure ship ever to sail the Pacific had left for Panama two weeks earlier. Her name was *Nuestra Señora*

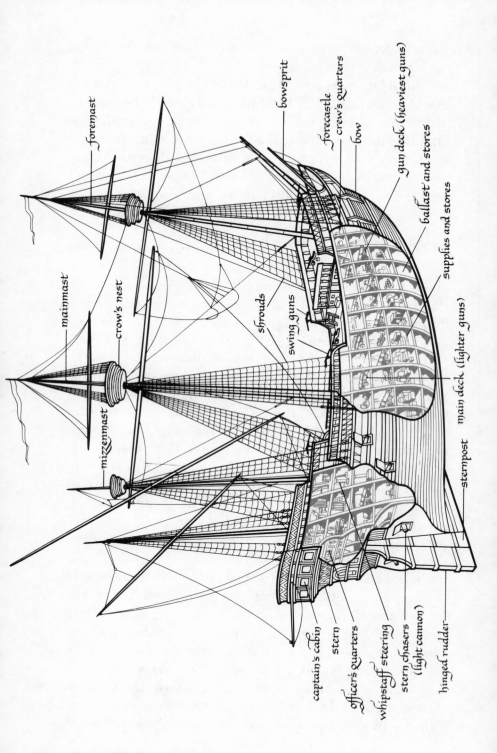

foremast

mainmast

crow's nest

mizzenmast

shrouds

swing guns

bowsprit

forecastle

crew's quarters

bow

gun deck (heaviest guns)

ballast and stores

supplies and stores

main deck (lighter guns)

sternpost

hinged rudder

stern chasers (light cannon)

whipstaff steering

officer's quarters

stern

captain's cabin

de la Concepcion,* but her sailors had nicknamed her *Cacafuego*, or *Spitfire*, because she carried many small cannon. These guns were no match for Drake's long-range cannon, but could do plenty of damage at close quarters.

The chase was on. Drake had every spare inch of sail unfurled until *Golden Hind*'s masts creaked and strained under their weight. High in the rigging lookouts scanned the horizon, eager for the gold chain that would go to the man who first saw the prize.

Cacafuego came into view just north of the Equator, near Ecuador. She was still far ahead, moving slowly. Why hurry? Wasn't the Pacific a Spanish lake?

Drake could have caught her easily, but that would have meant a battle, something he preferred to avoid whenever possible. *Cacafuego*'s captain was Juan de Anton, a tough, resourceful seaman whom it was best not to meet head-on. Surprise was the best tactic.

So as not to tip his hand, Drake had to gain on *Cacafuego*, although very slowly. Maybe the Spaniard felt so safe that he'd fall for an old trick? Drake ordered full sail, but also had a line of wine barrels filled with water strung out over the stern. These acted as a drag, so that *Golden Hind* looked like an overloaded merchantman making slow headway.

Juan de Anton watched curiously as the stranger slowly gained on him throughout the day. Maybe it brought a message from Peru, he thought. Curiosity finally got the best of him and, toward evening, he turned *Cacafuego* to meet the oncoming stranger. Drake's trap snapped shut.

As the ships approached, Drake cut the drag line, leaving the wine barrels behind. Instantly *Golden Hind* shot forward, drawing alongside the Spaniard. Juan de Anton shouted across, demanding the stranger's name and

---

* *Our Lady of the Conception*, named after the Virgin Mary.

destination. The words had hardly left his lips when he saw, staring up at him from the stranger's deck, some of the meanest looking sailors he had ever seen.

Drake's voice rang out. "We are English. Strike sail, Mr. Juan de Anton, or we will send you to the bottom."

"The devil take you English!" replied the proud Spaniard. "Come across yourselves and haul them down!"

His answer was the shrill sound of a whistle, the same whistle that had sounded from the jungle near the gold road.

A hail of musket balls swept across *Cacafuego*'s deck. A Spaniard fell with a howl of pain. Then another. And another.

Drake's cannon bellowed and *Cacafuego*'s mizzen-mast* toppled over the stern trailing a tangle of rope and canvas. By now boarders were swarming over the Spaniard's deck. The crew, taken by surprise by the fury of the assault, ran for safety belowdecks, leaving their captain alone with the enemy.

Dazed and trembling, Juan de Anton was hustled aboard *Golden Hind*. Drake smiled broadly and gently tapped his "guest" on the shoulder. "Don't be upset, my friend," said Drake. "Such are the fortunes of war."

After locking up the prisoners and putting his own men aboard the prize, Drake ordered both ships to head for the open ocean, where he intended to plunder the *Cacafuego*. Next morning, after a hearty breakfast, he went over the Spanish vessel with a fine-toothed comb.

Even Drake was amazed at his good fortune. Never had one ship given up so much treasure: bags full of precious stones, eighty pounds of gold, thirteen chests of silver coins, twenty-six *tons* of silver bars. As the loot was hoisted aboard *Golden Hind*, one Spaniard blurted out that *Spitfire* had become *Spitsilver*.

They were rich! Drake's backers would later receive fourteen hundred percent profit on their investment. The

---

* The mizzen is the third, or rear, mast of a three-masted sailing ship.

Caca Fogo.   Caca Plata.

The battle between the Golden Hind *(right) and the* Cacafuego, *renamed "Spitsilver" by a Spanish sailor because of the rich cargo the English took from its holds.*

share-out with his crew was equally generous. As the Spaniards looked on enviously, he distributed all of *Cacafuego*'s gold and silver plates, bowls, and goblets among his crew. Every man and boy got some valuable thing and, after putting his mark on it, returned it to Drake to be locked up for safekeeping until they reached home.

The Spaniards were now to be pleasantly surprised. Drake was a thief, but a generous one who always treated prisoners with kindness and respect. As soon as his own men were taken care of, he had the Spanish sailors lined up on *Cacafuego*'s deck. Each man then received a gift in keeping with his rank; Juan de Anton got a solid gold goblet engraved with the Latin name *"Franciscus Draques."* Finally he gave them their freedom, the greatest gift of all. Food was put aboard *Cacafuego* and the prisoners told they could sail wherever they wished.

Taking *Cacafuego*'s treasure was easy, compared with bringing it home safely. How should they return to England? Surely not by doubling back through the Straits of Magellan. No one wanted another taste of the storms of the far south. Besides, the Spaniards along the coast were on the alert and angry as hornets.

The only course left to them was to go home the long way, by sailing completely around the world. Luckily, Drake had captured a Spanish ship with a treasure as precious as its gold: detailed charts of the Pacific. With these as his guide, Drake sailed north along the coasts of Mexico and California. After taking on needed supplies near present-day San Francisco, he struck out across the Pacific. On September 26, 1580, *Golden Hind* dropped anchor off Plymouth after an absence of nearly three years.

England went wild with joy. Poets sang the praises of Drake, the first Englishman to circumnavigate the globe. Cheering crowds followed him everywhere, eager to get a glimpse of the hero. He became Queen Elizabeth's favorite. She proudly wore the diamond-studded cross he gave her and listened for hours to stories of his adventures.

Only the Spaniards were not amused. Their ambassador in London thundered against Drake, "the master thief of the known world." Any Christian ruler, he insisted, would execute such a criminal. Elizabeth listened politely, smiled sweetly, and spoke warmly of "my deare pyrat." Drake, of course, was no pirate, but the Queen's man doing her business. And everyone knew it.

Two months later, Queen Elizabeth and her court visited Drake aboard the *Golden Hind*. The ship was gaily decorated, as for a party. The crewmen cheered. Cannon thundered in salute. "Drake," she said in mock anger, "the King of Spain demands your head, and here I have a golden sword to strike it off."

She motioned for him to kneel, then, handing the sword to a nobleman, she had him touch Drake lightly on the shoulders with the flat of the blade. *"I bid thee rise, Sir Francis Drake!"* she said.

If the English thought of *Sir* Francis Drake as their greatest sea hero, the Spaniards saw him as a monster of evil. *"El Draque"* they called him: The Dragon. In the ports of Spain and the New World men whispered fearfully about his crystal ball, which revealed the location of every Spanish ship in the world. Drake was a witch, they said, an enemy of God and an ally of the Devil. If ever they caught him, he would be burned alive for witchcraft.

The Spaniards never came close to capturing him. England needed men like him in the war that now broke out between the two countries. No longer did Drake sail on his own to avenge personal injuries or with the backing of silent partners. He was the Queen's admiral, the boldest fighting man in England's cause.

He had left his bad luck behind him thirteen years earlier in the Panama jungle. Everything he tried succeeded no matter how dangerous it seemed. In 1585, he led twenty-nine warships to the New World, capturing the fortress-city of Santo Domingo on the island of Hispaniola and Cartagena, Colombia, at that time part of the Viceroyalty of Peru and the largest city on the Spanish Main. In 1587, he raided Cadiz, Spain, burning ships and supplies King Philip II had gathered for the invasion of England. The following spring, 1588, he was one of the admirals in charge of the fleet that defeated Spain's "Invincible Armada" in the English Channel.

Drake set out on his last voyage in August 1595. It was like old times, only now he shared command of a twenty-five-ship fleet with his cousin, John Hawkins. Their objective was a huge treasure ship known to be crippled in the harbor of San Juan, Puerto Rico.

By now, though, the commanders' lives had come around full-circle. Bad luck returned. The Spaniards had learned about the expedition in time to hide the treasure and beef up their defenses. A few days after arriving off Puerto Rico, disease broke out among the crews. Hawkins became ill and died. A few weeks later Drake, too, died and was buried at sea off Porto Bello, Panama, January 28, 1596.

When news of his death reached Spain, a visitor noted that "the joy of so much success has caused extreme satisfaction and rejoicing throughout the country. His Majesty shows the keenest delight and declares that the good news will help him get well rapidly."

He was wrong. For although the greatest of the sea rovers was gone, he could never be forgotten. The legend of Francis Drake lived on, and grew, becoming an inspiration to later generations. Soon others would be sailing in the wake of the *Golden Hind*.

<hr>

II

The Rise of the Buccaneers

Drake's successes were more than personal victories; they were signs of the weakening of Spanish power in Europe and the Americas. Although Spain still guarded her empire jealously, foreigners could not be kept out forever. The New World was too vast to be occupied and defended everywhere by Spaniards who were too few and too busy.

The West Indian Islands were one of the most important, yet also one of the weakest, Spanish possessions. Stretching from the Florida Keys to the Venezuelan coast, these islands extend for two thousand miles east and west across the Caribbean. Spain's first settlements in the New World were on the "Greater Antilles," the four largest islands of Cuba, Hispaniola (shared today by Haiti and the Dominican Republic), Puerto Rico, and Jamaica. Here slaves carved plantations out of the forests and looked after cattle and hogs brought from Europe. These colonies prospered until the 1520s, when many settlers left for the gold-rich territories of Mexico and Peru. The populations of the islands tumbled. Most of the smaller islands, or "Lesser Antilles," were deserted or never settled in the first place.

Foreigners—Englishmen, Frenchmen, Dutchmen— needed no invitation to take what the Spaniards couldn't

The Spanish Main and the West Indies
in the Age of the Sea Rovers

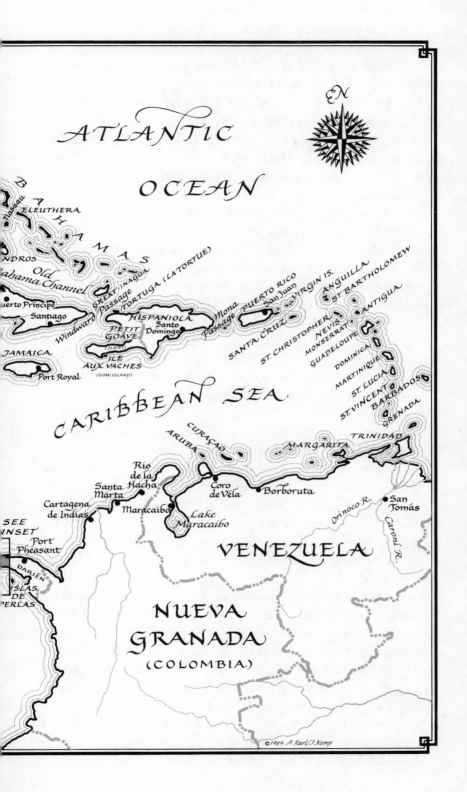

ATLANTIC

OCEAN

N

B
A
H
A
M
A
S

Nassau
ELEUTHERA
NDROS
Old
Bahama Channel
Puerto Principe
Santiago
JAMAICA
Port Royal

GREAT INAGUA
Windward Passage
TORTUGA (LA TORTUE)
HISPANIOLA
PETIT
GOAVE
Santo
Domingo
(HAITI)
ILE
AUX VACHES
(COW ISLAND)

Mona Passage
SANTA CRUZ
PUERTO RICO
San Juan
VIRGIN IS.
ANGUILLA
ST. BARTHOLOMEW
ST. CHRISTOPHER
NEVIS
MONSERRAT
GUADELOUPE
ANTIGUA
DOMINICA
MARTINIQUE
ST. LUCIA
ST. VINCENT
BARBADOS
GRENADA

CARIBBEAN SEA

CURAÇAO
ARUBA
MARGARITA
TRINIDAD

Rio
de la
Hacha
Santa
Marta
Cartagena
de Indias
Maracaibo
Coro
de Véla
Lake
Maracaibo
Borboruta
Orinoco R.
San
Tomás
Caroní R.

SEE
INSET
Port
Pheasant
DARIEN
ISLAS
DE
PERLAS

VENEZUELA

NUEVA
GRANADA
(COLOMBIA)

©1984 A. Karl/J. Kemp

or wouldn't use. Beginning in the early 1600s, small groups of adventurers settled on St. Christopher (St. Kitts), Nevis, Barbados, Antigua, and Montserrat. These islands seemed like Paradise to men used to the gray, weeping skies of northern Europe. Their offshore waters teemed with bass, tuna, and red snapper. Lobster and crab could be had for the taking from the tidal shallows. The flesh and eggs of the giant green sea turtle were a delicacy enjoyed even by slaves.

A regular trade developed between these trespassers and Europe. Ships brought new men and supplies, returning with cargoes of sugar, rum, and indigo, a valuable blue dye. It was from these islands and these ships that the buccaneers were recruited. For two centuries they and their descendants, the pirates, would bring terror and death to the Spanish lands bordering the Caribbean.

It all began innocently enough. Homeward bound English, French and Dutch vessels from North America would put in along the northern coast of Hispaniola for last-minute repairs before braving the Atlantic. Although thousands of Spaniards still lived in and around Santo Domingo in the south, this part of the island was nearly deserted. Haiti, the Indians called it—"The High Country," home of the Thunder Gods. All the landing parties found there were ruined plantations and the descendants of the farm animals left behind when the Spanish settlers moved away. Free to wander on their own, these animals quickly returned to the wild. And since they were without natural enemies, they multiplied until Haiti swarmed with cattle and pigs.

The ships' crews found it easy to kill a few animals for fresh meat to have during part of the ocean crossing. Sometimes men, singly or in small groups, jumped ship to take advantage of the easy pickings as fulltime hunters. The Indians taught them to preserve their meat in a special way. As soon as an animal was killed, it was skinned and the best cuts of meat sliced into long, narrow strips. These strips were laid over a grill and a fire started in bundles of green wood. The wood's dampness prevented the fire from becoming too hot and drying the meat too quickly. Waste fats, skin, and bone were slowly added to the fire, creating clouds of thick smoke. The result was an especially tasty piece of meat, red, like corned beef, that could keep for weeks. The Indians called the meat *bukan*. The hunters, most of whom were French, called themselves *boucaniers* (meat-curers), or in English "buccaneers."

The fame of *bukan* spread among seafarers. The meat was so delicious that captains sailed hundreds of miles out of their way to take in a supply. In exchange for some rough clothing, gunpowder, and bullets, they could stock up on enough of the delicacy for an entire voyage. Good food meant happy crews, and happy crews didn't mutiny.

The buccaneers' numbers grew along with their reputation. They came from many walks of life, but all had certain things in common. None was rich, or powerful, or of noble birth. One found in their ranks unemployed laborers and refugees from religious persecution. Many were criminals on the run. No one looked twice at a cow-killer with a big T, for "Thief," branded under his left eye close to the nose. Others were wanderers seeking their fortune anywhere in any way.

But most were sailors who had grown to hate the sea. Life for the ordinary seaman was nasty, dangerous, and short. None of the laws that protect seamen today existed until the 1800s. Sailing vessels were not designed for the crew's comfort, nor would merchants and governments spend more than the barest amounts for supplies. The best voyage, they believed, cost the least and earned the most. Too bad if half the crew died. There were always more poor men eager for a chance to work.

Cabins and bunks were for officers, not sailors. As darkness fell, those who were not on the night watch went below to the gun deck or the cargo holds. There each man lay down fully clothed on a piece of dirty sailcloth or sprawled on the rough floorboards. If water seeped in, as it usually did, he slept soaked to the skin. During cold spells, he slept shivering, or he didn't sleep at all, since blankets were too valuable to waste on sailormen.

Food was usually as bad as sleeping quarters. Rations quickly ran short, the remainder spoiling without refrigeration. "A sailor's stomach," the saying went, "could near digest iron." It had to if he didn't want to starve.

Undernourished men easily fell victim to disease. Water was too precious to waste on washing, which meant that crews had to go for months without cleaning themselves or their clothing. Toilet arrangements were simple: seats were slung over the deck rails fore and aft and everyone from captain to cabin boy did what he had to do in full public view. When the sea became too rough to use these seats, men used any out-of-the-way corner below. As a result, ships stank like sewers. Rats and cockroaches multiplied. Disease broke out sooner or later during every long voyage.

Shipboard discipline, too, was a killer. The law of the sea gave the captain complete control of his vessel. Disobeying even the craziest order was mutiny, punishable by death. Less serious crimes were dealt with more "mildly," although the culprit might still die. Lying was punished by the "Law of Moses," a few hundred lashes on the bare back with the cat-o'-nine-tails, a nine-stranded whip of knotted cords. A thief had a rope tied around his waist and was dropped into the sea three times from the top of the mainmast. They finally hoisted him up by the feet, half-drowned, to let the water run out of his stomach.

No wonder sailors deserted when they had the chance. Life among the buccaneers was hard, but not as hard as life aboard ship could be, and they were their own masters. They were not gentlemen. Mercy in battle, kindness to enemies, did not come naturally to them.

Never again would they see their people or their homelands. A new way of life had carved a channel deeper than any ocean between Europe and the High Country. Their people would not even have recognized them after a few weeks of the new life. They let their hair and beards grow into shaggy manes. Clothing was simple, consisting of peaked leather caps to protect the eyes from the sun and long shirts over trousers that reached midway between knees and ankles. Shoes were made by skinning a pig and putting bare feet into the wet leg skins; these were cut off above the ankle and tied with cord until they dried into "shoes." Buccaneers never changed a piece of clothing until it fell off in shreds. Most garments turned so black and stiff with the blood of slaughtered animals that they seemed to be covered with a thick layer of tar.

Theirs was a man's world, without room for wife or family. A buccaneer might live with an Indian or black woman for a while, but only for a little while. If he became serious about her, the others refused to go hunting with him.

The "Brothers of the Coast," as they called themselves, were happiest with one or two *matelots*, French slang for "mates" or "buddies." "Share and share alike" was their rule. If a *matelot* needed anything, he simply took it from his friend's pack without saying a word or having to replace it.

Buccaneers used their knives as easily as their hands. Each man carried three or four long, razor-sharp knives in his belt. The knife, not the gun, was his main hunting tool. Every morning before dawn a group of hunters set out on foot with a pack of fierce dogs they had tamed (mostly) from the wild. As soon as the dogs cornered a cow or bull, a hunter dashed forward. Dodging its slashing horns, he brought the animal down by cutting the muscles of its hind legs, then he cut its throat. Some of these hunters were so nimble that only two out of every hundred animals had to be shot.

The buccaneer's pride and joy was his musket. No ordinary gun, the "buccaneering-piece" was made by master gunsmiths in Nantes and Dieppe, France, for sale only in the High Country. These polished beauties, with their five-foot barrels, fired a one-ounce lead ball and kicked like a mule. The men behind these weapons were dead shots,

The best sharpshooter in the New World. A buccaneer smokes his pipe while standing guard with his long shovel-handled musket. Standing guard also are two of the half-wild dogs used to run down wild cattle and pigs.

the best marksmen this side of the Atlantic. Nobody in his right mind would dare to match them shot for shot.

For ten years nobody did challenge them. The Spaniards, of course, knew about them but looked the other way as long as their numbers remained small. Yet in time the Spanish authorities began to think these strangers were becoming too numerous and too close for comfort. They were already worried about the British, French and Dutch settlements in the Lesser Antilles. The Thirty Years' War raged in Europe, and the government feared that these settlements might become bases for attacks against the treasure fleets and towns of the Spanish Main.

Spanish war fleets were sent against the settlements,

driving the trespassers off Nevis and St. Kitts. Worse, soldiers were sent from Santo Domingo to deal with the buccaneers in the High Country. They were merciless, always striking silently and swiftly at night. Thus began the escalation of violence that would turn the Caribbean into a boiling cauldron. The buccaneers fought guerrilla-style, striking and running away before the enemy could catch his breath. Bands of *matelots* joined forces to ambush Spanish patrols and burn settlements.

The Spaniards replied with full-scale military expeditions to wipe out the hunters. When these failed, they began "search and destroy operations," as we call them today. While some soldiers searched for the buccaneers, others set out to destroy the animals they depended upon. At least half the wild cattle and pigs were slaughtered, their swollen carcasses left to rot in the tropical sun.

Buccaneer anger grew along with their determination not to give in. Lying a few miles off the northwest coast of Hispaniola is a small, rocky island. From the distance its brown-green color and hunchbacked shape make it seem like a gigantic turtle floating on the water. Hence its Spanish name, *Tortuga*—Turtle Island. Here, in 1630, the buccaneers joined refugees from the Lesser Antilles for safety and to plan their revenge. It would be war to the knife, war without pity.

In time a village of thatched-roofed huts grew along the beach near Tortuga's harbor. During the hunting season, groups of *matelots* set out across the channel for the main island and the familiar High Country. At season's end, they returned to Tortuga with fresh *bukan* to trade.

Yet times were changing. Not everyone returned; nor, indeed, did every buccaneer still hunt animals for a living. A few always remained in Hispaniola during the off season to waylay Spaniards. Some even gave up hunting altogether in favor of fighting the Spaniards full time. Among these were a handful of men who, remembering their sailor days, put out in canoes or tiny boats rigged with lateen (triangle-shaped) sails. But instead of heading for the open sea, they roamed the Hispaniola coast or hid in creeks waiting to pounce on unarmed Spanish craft.

Their attacks were bee stings to a mighty empire like Spain, but they hurt. Every few years, when the pain built up, Spanish fleets attacked Tortuga. A handful of buccaneers who weren't lucky enough or fast enough were killed or captured. Most, though, fled across the channel to hide in the forests they knew so well. When the Spaniards withdrew, they returned to pick up where they had left off.

By 1640, things had changed once again. Responsibility for this change goes to a man of daring and common sense. All we know of him is his first name—Peter—and his nationality—French. His last name was given by his fellow buccaneers: Le Grand. Pierre Le Grand, or Peter the Great.

Pierre had gone to Hispaniola in an open boat with twenty-eight men. Days passed without even a glimpse of a prize worth chasing. Their food almost gone, they knew they would have to return to Tortuga soon or starve. Pierre, however, had other plans. Tortuga lies at the southern end of the Old Bahama Channel between Cuba and the Bahama Islands. Since Columbus's day, ships bound for Spain had used this waterway with confidence; it was said to be as safe as the shores of the homeland itself. Pierre Le Grand changed all that.

Late one day, he saw a fleet of well-armed galleons plowing ahead in the distance. Trailing several miles behind was the largest vessel of all, which had somehow become separated from the group. Nobody aboard worried, or thought of catching up, because raiders never entered the Old Bahama Channel.

Pierre made up his mind to capture this prize or die trying. Slowly, quietly, under cover of the deepening darkness, the buccaneers gained on the towering galleon. To stiffen their courage, the captain had holes drilled in the bottom of the boat; the buccaneers would fight with redoubled courage, knowing there was no retreat if they failed.

Their boat was already sinking when it bumped against the galleon's side. Immediately everyone scrambled up the sides to the deck. So far so good. No guards. No gunners. No captain. No one but the lone helmsman dozing at his wheel. A knife jab put him to sleep forever.

The boarders ran to the stern cabin, where they found the ship's officers busy with a card game. "Jesus bless us!" the captain cried as Pierre held a pistol to his chest. "Are these devils, or what are they?" Other buccaneers, meanwhile, seized the gun room and took the rest of the crew prisoner. The "impossible" had happened. In a few minutes a handful of half-naked Frenchmen had captured a warship loaded with treasure in "safe" waters.

Pierre was not only brave and lucky, he knew that wise gamblers quit while they are ahead. After putting ashore the Spanish crewmen he didn't need, he made the others sail to France, where he released them, sold the prize and its cargo, and retired as a wealthy country gentleman.

News of Pierre's success rocketed from one end of the Caribbean to the other. Never before had so valuable a prize been taken so easily by so few. The Spaniards were shocked, vowing revenge. The buccaneers were overjoyed, each man vowing to outdo Pierre. Hunting wild cattle was nearly forgotten in the rush to go sea roving. After forty years, the sailors returned to the sea.

◆◆

Tortuga became a magnet drawing adventurers from the Caribbean islands and beyond. Frenchmen, always in the majority, rubbed shoulders with English, Scots, Irish, Dutch, and Portuguese buccaneers. Here, too, came blacks with whiplash scars crisscrossing their backs, and somber Massachusetts men unhappy with the Puritan rulers of the Bay Colony.

The seagoing buccaneers were a strange breed. Drake and Hawkins had sailed with the blessing and backing of royalty; they commanded disciplined crews and fought according to the laws of war of their day. The buccaneers had no ruler's support. They recognized no rules of war except those they made for themselves.

Buccaneers were not common criminals or pirates. The law said pirates were "enemies of the human race." Every ship, regardless of the flag it flew, was fair game to be attacked anytime. Buccaneers, though, were fussy thieves. The Brethren of the Coast welcomed everyone— everyone who wasn't Spanish. Ninety-nine out of a hundred times they would allow a ship to pass—as long as it wasn't Spanish. Spain was their enemy, the target of their burning hatred. All others could feel safe anywhere in the Caribbean.

The buccaneers governed themselves by a strict set of rules called The Custom of the Coast. Although these rules were not set down in law books, the Brethren knew them as well as they knew their own names. According to custom, "articles" were drawn up before a voyage for everyone to sign with his name or mark, an X or other design if he couldn't write. These articles were really a constitution spelling out everyone's role, responsibilities, and rewards.

Moviemakers and novelists have often shown the buccaneer captain as a cruel tyrant. Cruel he might be, but never a tyrant. A buccaneer vessel was really a floating democracy. The crewmen had suffered enough under regular ships' officers to trust someone ever again with such power. Their captains were elected by majority vote, serving only as long as they kept their crew's confidence.

The captain was chosen for his sailing skill, fighting ability, and luck. His word was law during battle, obeyed instantly and without question. But when the ship was not in action, he was like anyone else on board. No silver plates or music for him at mealtimes. Nor did he give orders. It was better to save his breath, since no one would listen to him anyhow. The crew decided through discussion and voting how to run the ship. The captain did as his men wished, or was dismissed.

Yet discipline aboard a buccaneer vessel was strict,

punishments usually deadly. A sneak thief, for instance, was given fair warning. The first offense cost him an ear or his nose. A second offense brought "marooning." The culprit was marooned—stranded—on one of the hundreds of tiny desert islands that dot the Caribbean. He was given a bottle of water, some bread, and a loaded pistol. Days later, when hunger and thirst became unbearable, the pistol gave him a quick way out.

Articles also mentioned how the loot was to be divided. "No prey, no pay" was the rule in money matters. Nobody was entitled to a reward just for coming along. If no prizes were taken, well, that was just too bad. Whatever loot that did come their way was divided into portions, or shares. Everyone got something, although not the same amount. The captain, as war leader, was allowed five shares to the ordinary sailor's one. The ship's doctor, gunner, and carpenter claimed two or three shares each, because of their special skills.

The buccaneers invented a type of accident insurance to aid those who were wounded in action. Different injuries were worth different amounts. Loss of the right hand was most serious, since the buccaneer couldn't earn a living without his sword hand. Anyone so crippled received six hundred pieces of eight, Spanish silver coins worth about three dollars in today's money. A lost leg brought four hundred to five hundred pieces of eight. You could still fight on a wooden leg, and "Peg-leg" was a popular nickname aboard buccaneer ships. A missing finger or eye was a minor handicap worth only one hundred pieces of eight. A black patch over an eye was a badge of honor in the taverns of Tortuga.

Before going to sea, each man brought aboard his share of gunpowder and bullets. Food was no problem, not with such fine *bukan* available. As an added treat, the buccaneers captured giant tortoises, some over a hundred years old, which were laid on their back below decks. Tortoises can live for weeks in this position, a ready source of fresh meat.

The skills of guerrilla warfare learned in the High Country easily carried over to the Caribbean. At sea, as on land, boldness and speed were equalizers against a larger enemy. The buccaneers favored the sloop, an open sailing boat of about twenty-five tons, for their raids. Although tiny next to a galleon, the sloop was more than a match for the warship. It handled like a dream, answering the helmsman's slightest touch on the wheel. Lying low in the water, it could be hidden behind small islands and approach a victim without standing out against the horizon. The single lateen sail used every breath of wind to overtake an enemy and dodge his gunfire.

Ability to dodge was all-important, since buccaneer craft were always outgunned by Spanish warships. A sloop carried no more than six light cannon; a galleon mounted at least thirty heavy cannon on each side. These cannon fired different kinds of shot, depending upon the kind of damage the captain wanted to do to an enemy. Solid iron balls could break a ship to pieces. Bar shot, a smaller version of a weightlifter's barbells, tumbled through the air with the force of a buzz saw. It could tear sails and rope lines to shreds, or rip a man apart. For close work there was grape shot, canvas bags filled with musket balls that sprayed an enemy with a hailstorm of lead. "Angrage" sounds like "anger" and "rage"; it was a devil's mixture of nails, nuts, bolts, chain, and odd scraps of metal that blew across an enemy's deck.

A gunnery duel against such odds would have meant suicide for the buccaneers. During an approach, the sloop's helm was turned over to a "sea artist," the captain or crewman most skilled in ship-handling. The sea artist relied upon darkness to come as close to his victim as possible without coming under cannon fire. The best time to attack was before dawn or sunset, when a small vessel was barely visible but a large one easily seen.

The sea artist really earned his extra shares if the galleon's lookouts were on the job. From the distance the buccaneers could hear the ship's drummers beating the call

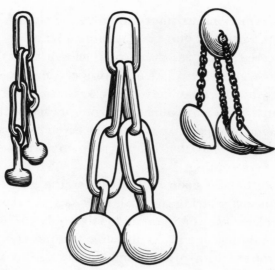

CHAIN SHOT
Different kinds of shot were used for different situations. Solid cannon balls made holes in the enemy's hull. Chain shot spun through the air like a buzz saw to cut the sails and ropes of an enemy ship. The chain shot at the right is made with sharp blades, useful against enemy sailors as well as their ship.

to battle stations. Long battle streamers were unfurled at the mast tops. The Spanish captain tried desperately to turn his vessel broadside to the oncoming sloop to allow his guns to fire all at once. But the sea artist was wise to that game. He kept his attention riveted on the ship ahead, following its every twist and change of course. Whatever it did, the sloop did that instant. As long as he kept on her stern, she could not turn to deliver her crushing broadside.

The only cannon the buccaneers had to worry about were the four light pieces in the galleon's stern. Now their skill with the musket paid off. Standing in the bow of the sloop was the best marksman in the crew. The sloop pitched and rolled, but he kept his eyes glued to the galleon's gun ports. Whenever the small wooden doors opened to permit gunners to take aim, he aimed and fired first. His motions were quick, precise, mechanical. His musket's crack was nearly always followed by a shriek of pain. Without turning, he reached back for a freshly loaded weapon, which an assistant placed in his hand. The firing continued until the gun ports slammed shut.

The sea artist eased his craft closer to the galleon, which rose up in front like a floating castle. The sloop slid into the watery valley between two waves, while the galleon climbed the wave ahead, growing larger in the fading light. Wind wailed. Canvas rustled. Wet wood squeaked. White water rushed by, leaving a foamy wake. The buccaneers were gaining.

At last their sloop nestled under the galleon's overhanging stern. Staring upward, they saw the painted coat of arms of the king of Spain and elaborately carved designs on the moldings. Lanterns flickered behind the tall windows wrapped in a row around the stern. But their first objective lay directly in front: the galleon's hinged rudder secured to the sternpost. The Spaniard's hope of escape remained alive only so long as that rudder stayed in working order.

Time was running out for the galleon. The buccaneer sharpshooter and his assistants moved back to the stern, making room for others in the bow. Their replacements were also specialists, only their weapons were large wooden wedges and mallets. As one man held a wedge in place, his partner raised the mallet over his head with both hands, driving it in solidly between rudder and sternpost. Two wedges secured. Three. Four. The galleon's sails billowed, but she no longer obeyed the helmsman's commands. Her rudder was jammed. She was helpless.

The buccaneers tensed, waiting for the signal to go into action. The captain raised his arm, then brought it down sharply. "Boarders away!" he shouted.

Without warning, the Spaniards nearest the sloop heard an eerie swishing sound. Below, men twirled grapnels attached to ropes over their heads in ever-widening circles. Grapnels resemble huge four-pronged fish hooks for grabbing something and holding it tight.

One after another grapnels caught the taffrail, the upper part of the galleon's stern. Above the roar of the sea

Preparing to board. A barefooted buccaneer begins to twirl a four-pronged grapnel that will fasten onto a Spanish treasure ship.

came the wild shouts of buccaneers shinnying up the ropes. Glass shattered as boarders broke through the stern cabin windows. Others, meanwhile, bellied over the taffrail.

Stripped to the waist and barefooted for better traction, they looked even more terrible than they sounded. Experienced soldiers, who didn't scare easily, shook in their shoes as they saw the buccaneers up close for the first time. For many it would also be the last time.

Each buccaneer was a walking arsenal, armed literally to the teeth. The heavy muskets had been left behind in favor of smaller guns for close-in work. Some boarders carried the blunderbuss, a shortbarreled musket that fired

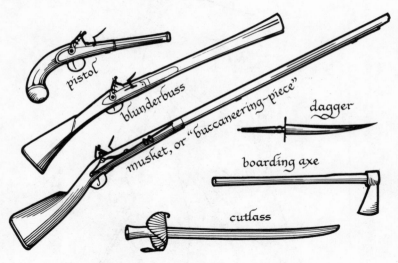

pistol

blunderbuss

musket, or "buccaneering-piece"

dagger

boarding axe

cutlass

TOOLS OF THE SEA ROVERS' TRADE

many small slugs like a modern shotgun. But no buccaneer was truly dressed for work without two, and as many as six, pistols held in holsters attached to a leather sling worn across the shoulders. Although the pistol of the 1600s fired only one bullet, it was deadly even when empty. A skillful fighter knew how to use an empty pistol as a club or missile to be flung into an enemy's eyes.

Buccaneers were also experienced bomb makers. Hand grenades, or "grenados," were simple but effective weapons. An old wine bottle was filled with gunpowder and rusty iron scraps, which scattered in all directions when set off by a fuse. "Smoke screens" were made by igniting clay jars filled with yellow sulphur, a chemical that gives off clouds of blinding smoke and a sickening odor of rotten eggs, only many times stronger.

The weapons the buccaneer most depended upon for victory in close combat were his blades. In addition to the three or four hunting knives in his belt, he had a boarding axe. This weapon was similar to the American Indian tomahawk, although heavier. It could be used for cracking skulls as well as smashing through cabin doors. Finally,

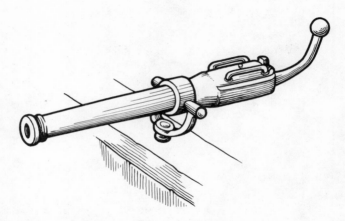

The swivel gun, a small cannon that could be loaded and fired by one man, was used to repell boarders.

there was the cutlass, a short, heavy sword, slightly curved to permit slashing. A single blow with a cutlass could lop off a man's arm, or head, without any trouble.

Buccaneers were not sportsmen who believed in giving an enemy an even chance. Their idea of a fair fight was to do anything that let them win. Some men really "used their heads"—to butt an opponent in the stomach. Others bit him anywhere they could. A few blinded opponents by spitting streams of bitter tobacco juice into their eyes.

The Spaniards prepared to throw back boarders as best they could. Men with eight-foot spears called "boarding pikes" took positions on deck, next to swordsmen and musketeers. In front of them the portion of deck over which the buccaneers had to come was made slippery with hog grease or moistened soap; bushels of peas served the same purpose. Tacks and broken bottles were scattered to cut the invaders' bare feet.

Ignoring their wounds, which many didn't even feel in the excitement of battle, the buccaneers swarmed across the deck. The battle became a disorganized chaos, a swirl of action. The defenders' discipline began to break down under the reckless fury of the assault. That recklessness, too, had a good reason behind it, for only in a wild free-

Pirates "sweating a prisoner." The prisoner was jabbed with spears and forced to run around the mast until he collapsed; then he was killed.

Drink up—or else! A pirate forces a prisoner to drink a full quart of rum at one swallow. This or a bullet were his only choices.

for-all could the outnumbered boarders throw the enemy off balance.

Not every Spaniard had to be killed in order to capture the ship—only most of the officers, without whom the crew became a leaderless mob. At first one by one, then in small groups, they dropped their weapons and raised their hands. Now their sufferings truly began.

The buccaneers' reputation for cruelty to prisoners was true only in part. Everything depended upon their past experiences with Spaniards and their losses in taking the ship. If they had been treated well, the ship was looted, its masts cut down, and the passengers and crew told to sail it to a friendy port as best they could. More often they had been mistreated, or the Spaniards defended the vessel too stubbornly. In that case only God could help the prisoners.

The buccaneers were as inventive in their cruelties as in their fighting style. Male captives might be hung from the yards by their thumbs and shot for target practice, or tortured with lumps of hot charcoal. Women who did not have wealthy relatives to ransom them were tossed to the sharks or sold into slavery on the sugar plantations in the Lesser Antilles.

———◆•◆———

Although as many as two thousand buccaneers may have been roaming the Caribbean by the 1650s, the names of just a few have come down to us. These men were not interested in being remembered by future generations. Rough, brutal fellows, they lived for the moment. Tomorrow, let alone next week or next year, was too far to think about. "Easy come, easy go" could have been their motto along with "no prey, no pay." No matter how much loot they took, it slipped through their fingers like grains of sand. At Tortuga men gambled and drank away hundreds of pieces of eight and gold doubloons, coins worth about thirty dollars in today's money. Then, bleary-eyed, their pockets turned inside out, they staggered down the beach in search of new articles to sign.

Portrait of Bartolomeo the Portuguese from Esquemeling's The Buccaneers of America *of 1684. Bartolomeo was a fierce fighter who led many battles at sea.*

If we remember any of these men it is because of a French adventurer named John Esquemeling. As a young man, Esquemeling found his way to Tortuga, where he became fascinated with the buccaneers, whose story he set down in a book first published in Dutch in 1678 and in English six years later: *The Buccaneers of America; A True Account of the Remarkable Assaults Committed of Late Years upon the Coasts of the West Indies by the Buccaneers of Jamaica and Tortuga, Both English and French.* In spite of its long-winded title, Esquemeling's book is the best eyewitness account we have of the lives of the buccaneers.

The Brethren of the Coast told Esquemeling about the Frenchman Montbars, nicknamed "The Exterminator," whose sense of justice turned him into a heartless killer. Montbars hated the Spaniards for enslaving the Indians. Nothing gave him greater pleasure than torturing them in revenge. One day Montbars, his ship and his crew disappeared at sea without a trace.

Bartolomeo the Portuguese was born in Portugal, coming to the New World as a teenager. He seemed to have nine lives, for no sooner did the Spaniards capture him than he escaped. His escapes were all the more amazing because he couldn't swim.

Bartolomeo once fell into Spanish hands when his ship ran aground on the Mexican coast. The governor had made up his mind to hang him the next day and, to make sure he didn't escape, locked him up aboard a ship. That night he stabbed the guard with a knife he had hidden under his clothes and floated ashore with a pair of "water wings" made of empty wine jugs. A week later he returned with some buccaneer cronies to steal the very ship that had been his prison. But by then his luck had run out. The vessel was wrecked off Cuba and he never captured another.

Jean-David Nau, known as L'Olonnois after his hometown of Sable d' Olonne, France, was the most inhuman of

L'Olonnoise the Cruel taught buccaneers to capture whole cities rather than single ships. Indians he had previously mistreated tortured him to death after his ship ran aground.

the buccaneers. The mention of his name, people said, was enough to empty towns in his path. Even snakes were supposed to slither into the jungle when he came near.

The Frenchman earned his nickname of "L'Olonnois the Cruel." He once had eighty-seven prisoners tied and placed on the ground in a row. Sword in hand, he walked down the line, stopping only to cut off each man's head. "His cruelties against the Spaniards," Esquemeling says, "were such that the very fame of them made him known through the whole Indies. For which reasons the Spaniards chose to die or sink fighting than surrender."

L'Olonnois, like Pierre Le Grand earlier, changed the nature of buccaneering. The Brethren of the Coast had been satisfied to attack Spanish shipping, avoiding the well-defended mainland settlements. L'Olonnois thought these tactics stupid and wasteful. Instead of trying to pick off one prize at a time, he talked six hundred buccaneers into joining him with their ships. Never before had the Spaniards faced such a threat in the New World. For with such a powerful fleet, the Frenchman had the cities of the Spanish Main at his mercy. He showed no mercy. In the spring of 1667, his men looted the wealthy cities of Maracaibo and Gibraltar, Venezuela, killing hundreds of innocent men, women, and children.

L'Olonnois's career ended about a year later on the Panama coast after his ship broke up in a storm. The Indians, Esquemeling says, "took him prisoner and tore him to pieces alive, throwing his body limb by limb into the fire and his ashes into the air; to the intent no trace nor memory might remain of such an inhuman creature." That his memory does remain is due to the buccaneer author John Esquemeling.

And yet, strange as it seems, L'Olonnois and the other Tortuga captains were beginners at buccaneering alongside the Welshman who now stepped onto the stage.

——— ◆•◆ ———

III

Henry Morgan, The Buccaneer Prince

You knew it the moment you saw him: something about Henry Morgan set him apart from the waterfront crowds of Port Royal, Jamaica, in the late 1600s. Here was a man who knew how to give orders and who expected to be obeyed.

Not that he was especially handsome, or fashionably dressed. Of average height, weighing one hundred and seventy-five pounds, he had the arms and shoulders of one used to physical labor outdoors. His broad, unsmiling face was clean-shaven except for a long mustache that fluffed out at the ends and a tuft of hair, hardly a beard, in the crease beneath the lower lip. Portraits show him with a shoulder-length wig, which he wore only on special occasions, because the masses of curls made him miserable in the tropical heat. He usually went hatless, his close-cropped hair covered with a red bandanna. The rest of his outfit included a silk vest, knee-length pantaloons, cotton stockings, and buckled shoes. A silver-handled sword dangled from his hip. A pistol decorated with ivory and gold was thrust in his belt within easy reach.

Townspeople lowered their voices, bowing their heads slightly as he passed. No one told them how to behave.

With his long curls and fancy clothes, Henry Morgan seems to be a peace-loving gentleman. But the burning ships in the background tell us that Morgan was the buccaneer prince of Jamaica.

The most ignorant ruffian knew what was proper in the presence of such a man. He radiated authority. His hard, gray-blue eyes, the self-assurance of his movements, made him seem princely. Henry Morgan *was* a prince of sorts—the buccaneer prince of the Caribbean.

It hadn't always been this way. Morgan had risen quickly in the world since he first arrived in the islands. The most famous of the buccaneers was born in Wales about 1635, the son of Robert Morgan, a prosperous farmer. Little is known of his early life, except that staying on a quiet farm in an out-of-the-way corner of Great Britain did not appeal to him. Thoughts of America, with its promises of adventure and wealth, quickened his blood until he could wait no longer. And so, when nearly twenty he sold himself as an indentured servant; that is, his passage to the New World was paid in return for his "indenture," or contract, to work on a plantation for three years. Morgan served his term in Barbados, where he found farm work even less to his liking than at home. He gritted his teeth and bent his back, waiting for the moment of freedom. When his indenture expired, he took ship for Jamaica.

Of all the Spanish colonies, Jamaica alone had been captured and held by another European power. In 1655, during another of the wars between the two countries, a British fleet landed troops on the island, easily defeating its Spanish defenders. Admiral William Penn, the fleet's commander, is remembered less for his victory than as the father of the founder of Pennsylvania, a man of peace who believed drawing the sword to be against God's law.

Admiral Penn's countrymen had much need of swordsmen during their early years in Jamaica. A glance at the map will show that this island is a clenched fist aimed at Cuba, Hispaniola, and the treasure cities of the Spanish Main. The Spaniards' worst nightmare had come true. No matter what the cost, Jamaica had to be retaken.

They almost succeeded several times—*almost*! The British government, faced with troubles in Europe, withdrew its naval squadrons from the Caribbean, leaving only a handful of tired, diseased troops to defend Jamaica. Spanish battle fleets would easily have recaptured it had not the island's governors used their only resource: the buccaneers.

Whenever spies reported the Spaniards gathering for an attack, Jamaica's governor sent out a call for help. The buccaneers rushed to answer the call, not only because they hated Spain, but because they welcomed the chance to become privateers. The privateer waged "private war." For centuries European governments had issued "letters of marque and reprisal" whenever their navies were too small or too busy to deal with a certain enemy. These letters named the enemy and licensed the privateer to seize his property whenever possible. Anyone with the means could outfit a ship, hire a crew, and attack, knowing that he would be treated as a war prisoner rather than a pirate if captured. A letter of marque and reprisal was actually a valuable hunting license.

English buccaneers leaped at the chance to go to Jamaica, especially since the French majority wanted to push them out of Tortuga. At last they had a base that belonged to a lawful government. Besides, even in time of peace, without letters of marque and reprisal, the governors could be counted on to look the other way if they came ashore with Spanish loot.

Jamaica became a buccaneer's paradise. Next to its helpful governors, its best feature was a vast harbor in the south. Protected by the Palisadoes, a low, nine-mile-long sandspit running parallel to the shore, this harbor is one of the five or six finest in the world. Hundreds of ships at a time have ridden out hurricanes nestled safely behind this natural shield.

At the tip of the Palisadoes, between the harbor's mouth and the sea, the English built Port Royal. Although not much of a town compared to those in Europe, Port Royal throbbed with life. Its streets were merely narrow paths ankle-deep with mud and filth. They stank, but no one seemed to care or to be bothered by the inconvenience. There was too much money to be made to bother about "little things" like dirt.

The dirtiest street ran along the waterfront. Having a house here guaranteed even the laziest merchant a fortune within a year. For plunder was Port Royal's chief industry, and the waterfront street lay a few steps away from the pebbly beach where returning buccaneer ships unloaded. Silks, spices, gemstones, spools of silver and gold thread, laces, rare woods, bales of fine tobacco, perfumes, ornate furniture, bags of pearls: everything was heaped up helter-

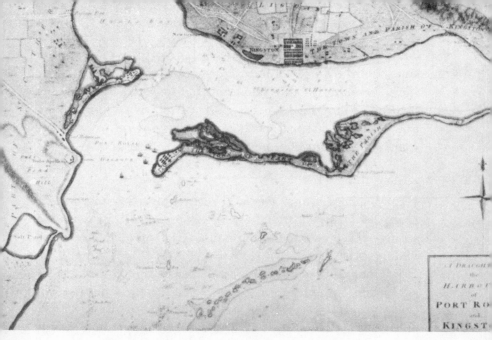

A map dating from the 1700s shows Kingston harbor, Jamaica, with Port Royal at the tip of the long sandspit known as the Palisadoes.

skelter and sold at auction for one-hundredth of its true value.

Easy come, easy go. Their pockets already heavy with pieces of eight and doubloons, buccaneers weren't worried about being cheated. The goods put ashore were the "left-overs," the hard-to-carry booty. Anyhow, why should they care? Weren't there always more prizes, richer prizes, waiting to be taken?

Port Royal was reckoned the wickedest spot on earth. More people were killed in street brawls here in a year than in the whole of Scotland. Here were to be found more taverns than in London; indeed, there was one tavern for every ten men.

Yet one didn't have to buy drinks in a tavern. Alcohol flowed in the streets. Townspeople often met drunken sailors out on a spree. One man wore expensive breeches of purple velvet, with a plumed hat balanced crazily on his head; gold hoop earrings dangled from his pierced ears. Standing in front of him in the middle of the street was a

Henry Morgan, The Buccaneer Prince   63

one hundred twenty-five-gallon barrel of wine, its top smashed in by a pistol butt. He shouted rather than sang a song, demanding between verses that passersby drink to his health—or else, for he pointed the pistol menacingly. Now and then he cupped his hands to fling wine at women, roaring with laughter as it stained their dresses.

◆◆◆

Henry Morgan, age twenty-three, made his home among these people. Not that he ever lost control; he was too strong-willed ever to cut loose in a wild spree. He saved his violence for "business."

Upon arriving in Jamaica, Morgan signed the articles of the first outgoing buccaneer vessel he could find. During this and other voyages, he became known for his courage, cleverness, and coolness in the face of danger. No doubt about it: young Morgan was a good fellow to have on your side in a tight spot.

Morgan also showed himself to be a good business-man. He saved his prize money until there was enough to buy a small vessel in partnership with some friends. Naturally the crew elected him captain.

During the next six years Morgan scoured the Carib-bean, until Spaniards began to whisper that Drake had returned from the grave to haunt them. He never seemed to make a serious mistake or outrun his luck. His reputa-tion grew until, in 1664, he met Edward Mansvelt, a wily Dutchman who commanded a fleet of fifteen buccaneer vessels. Mansveld recognized the younger man's abilities, inviting him to become his second-in-command with the title of Vice-Admiral. Before he died in 1667, Mansvelt had taught Morgan all he knew about attacking settle-ments along the Spanish Main and leading large numbers of ships in battle.

Mansvelt's death was the turning point in Morgan's career. The buccaneer crews, meeting in solemn council, elected him Admiral. Several weeks later, Sir Thomas Modyford, Governor of Jamaica, named him chief of the

Exhorting Tribute From the Citizens, *a painting by Howard Pyle. The mayor of a Spanish town, on his knees, knows what will happen if he doesn't tell where the treasure is hidden. Although Pyle lived three centuries later, his pictures of buccaneer and pirate life are as accurate as they are beautiful.*

island's privateers with a commission to attack Spanish ships and settlements. He needed no further encouragement.

The years 1668–1670 saw Spain's American empire assaulted as never before. Drake himself would have been surprised at Morgan's boldness. But would he have been proud? Certainly not. For *El Draque* never harmed the innocent, never ordered the cruelties that Morgan believed were a normal part of war.

Morgan's first large-scale expedition was against Puerto Principe, Cuba, early in 1668. The results were disappointing, for although the town fell after a fierce battle, the loot wasn't worth the efforts of 750 men sailing in twenty ships. He'd have to do better or risk losing his men's loyalty. Already buccaneers were grumbling, vowing never to follow him again.

In June, Morgan set out to win back their respect by capturing Porto Bello on the coast of Panama. Porto Bello, or "the lovely port," was an important trading center where merchants from Spain and the colonies met to do business. Moreover, ever since Drake's raid on Nombre de Dios nearly 100 years before, the treasure-carrying mule trains had been sent twenty miles to the west to the king's treasure house in Porto Bello.

The Spaniards had planned wisely. In addition to its beauty, Porto Bello was strongly defended. Although it was not surrounded by walls, the town lay at the far end of a harbor resembling a narrow-mouthed sack. High on the cliffs on each side of the entrance was a castle whose walls bristled with heavy cannon. Any invaders would be caught in a cross-fire and blown to bits. Jutting into the harbor from the town itself, and joined to it by a narrow bridge, was the third and largest castle, Santiago de la Gloria.

Morgan sailed with four hundred fifty men in nine ships, making sure not to mention their destination until well out to sea. The crews were shocked when he broke the news. Their faces flushed with anger, men shouted that they were too few and poorly armed to challenge such defenses.

Mutiny seemed certain until Morgan showed himself to be as good at speechmaking as fighting. Flattery, he knew, could sometimes do more than threats. He reminded his men that although their numbers were small, their hearts were large: brave men don't turn back without firing a shot. Besides, the fewer buccaneers who came along, the larger would be each man's share of the loot. The men cheered, vowing to follow Morgan anywhere. For years afterwards, sailors sang Morgan's words:

> *If few there be amongst us,*
> *Our hearts are very great;*
> *And each will have more plunder,*
> *And each will have more plate.*

Morgan believed in doing the unexpected, in attacking where the enemy felt safest. Instead of sailing under the castle's guns, he decided to attack at night from the rear. After a stormy crossing of the Caribbean, his ships dropped anchor at the mouth of a small river west of Porto Bello. Skeleton crews were left behind with orders to sail to the town next day, while he set out overland on foot with the main force.

The invaders were guided by an Englishman who had been a prisoner in Porto Bello and knew every inch of the jungle to the west. Morgan planned to capture the castle at the harbor's western entrance, leaving its companion on the opposite shore isolated and out of the battle.

The buccaneers marched along winding jungle trails, ghostly shadows moving in the moonlight. Hours later, they took up positions at the edge of a clearing across from the castle. On top of the walls, outlined against the sky, guards walked to and fro on their rounds. A Spanish soldier captured along the way was made to shout Morgan's message to the garrison: surrender or die. The answer came in a burst of gunfire.

The buccaneers broke from cover at a run. Within minutes the shouting, cutlass-swinging mob heaved its grapnels and had swarmed over the wall. It was just like taking a ship, only easier, because there were no waves to throw the "boarders" off balance.

The battle for the main fort at Portobello, Panama. As grenades are hurled by attackers and defenders, Morgan's buccaneers climb the ladders brought to the walls by priests and nuns, many of whom were shot by the defenders.

Morgan now kept his promise. Coolly, matter-of-factly, he had the prisoners locked in a room above the magazine, the castle's ammunition room. Ordering his men to safety, he had the gunpowder set off with a long fuse. A mighty explosion shattered the night, followed by a fireball that lit up the road into the town like the noonday sun.

The buccaneers swept across the castle's smoking ruins into the town. Panic gripped the people of Porto Bello. Most ran about aimlessly in their nightclothes, not knowing what to do or where to go. The wealthier citizens threw their jewels and money down wells and into water storage tanks for safety. About one hundred people, led by the town governor, fled to the castle of Santiago de la Gloria.

The governor, a man named Castellón, was a brave warrior whose sense of honor would never allow him to give up a place entrusted to him by the king of Spain. As soon as the castle's heavy wooden doors slammed shut, he ordered the guns to open fire on the town. Cannon balls whizzed overhead, not caring who they struck. They mowed down citizens and buccaneers alike.

Morgan, calm as ever, gave his orders. Sharpshooters fired at the gunners atop the walls. Men with grapnels rushed forward, to be met by showers of boiling water, flaming tar, and exploding grenades. From daybreak to noon the buccaneers attacked, only to be driven off with heavy losses. Morgan was beginning to lose hope of taking the castle when he had an idea. He ordered his carpenters to make a dozen ladders wide enough for four men to climb side by side.

But who would carry these ladders to the wall? Not the buccaneers, who already had a healthy respect for Castellón's leadership ability.

Morgan had the answer, although not the one any honorable soldier then or now would consider. He decided to use prisoners as human shields for his assault parties. Scores of priests and nuns were rounded up in the churches and brought to the battlefield. There they were forced to pick up the ladders and walk toward the walls, each with a buccaneer behind his or her back. Surely the governor would not shoot down innocent religious people, they thought.

How wrong they were! Castellón ordered his soldiers to open fire at close range. Cannon roared, sending iron balls into groups of people below. Many fell dead or wounded, their places filled by others until the ladders rested against the wall. With a whoop and a holler, the buccaneers sprang to the attack.

The Spaniards fought bravely until it became clear

that resistance was useless. Only Castellón refused to surrender. His sword flashed, cutting down any buccaneer who dared approach.

Morgan's men could easily have shot him, had not their chief called them off. Cruel as he was, Morgan admired bravery. And this Spaniard was the bravest man he'd ever seen. It would be a shame to kill him, Morgan thought.

But Castellón was too proud (some said too foolish) to "dishonor" himself with surrender. "I had rather die as a valiant soldier than be hanged as a coward," he shouted. Morgan nodded, a little sadly, and the buccaneers shot the brave Spaniard with pistols.

The battle over, Morgan's ships sailed into the beautiful port, making sure to steer clear of the undamaged castle on the eastern shore. For fifteen days the buccaneers terrorized Porto Bello's citizens. Finding the king's treasure house empty, they tortured men, women, and children to make them reveal where their family valuables were hidden. Many told. Many poor people died because they had nothing to reveal.

Meanwhile the governor of Panama had set out across the isthmus with several hundred soldiers in the hope of trapping the buccaneers. He was trapped instead. As the Spaniards entered a narrow ravine, a hundred buccaneer marksmen opened fire at once, sending them running for their lives.

The next day a Spanish messenger arrived at Morgan's camp under a white flag of truce. In his pocket was one of the strangest messages ever sent by one soldier to another. His master, His Excellency the Governor of Panama, congratulated the buccaneer chief on taking so mighty a city with so few men. He would appreciate it very much if Morgan could send him a sample of the weapons his men had used in gaining the victory.

Morgan grinned, half in amusement, half in mockery. Of course he'd give the noble gentleman a pistol and some lead balls. Let the governor study them carefully, as they were only a loan. For in exactly a year Morgan would come to "Penamaw," as he called it, to take them back.

The governor immediately sent back the weapons with a valuable gold ring and a message. The ring was a gift for Morgan's courtesy. The message was a warning that he should stay away from Panama City if he valued his life. Morgan laughed, slipped the ring on his finger, and sailed away with loot worth over three hundred thousand pieces of eight taken.

◆••◆

Back at Port Royal, the buccaneers drank deeply and gambled carelessly while their money lasted, which wasn't for long. Just as they were growing restless, in January 1669, word came that Morgan was gathering a force at Cow Island, a deserted island off Hispaniola's south coast. The conqueror of Porto Bello had no trouble signing up all the fighting men he needed.

A freak accident almost ended the expedition before it began. Among the vessels at Cow Island was the *Oxford*, a three hundred-ton beauty of thirty-six guns sent by Jamaica's governor to be Morgan's flagship. One evening the admiral called a meeting of captains in the *Oxford*'s great cabin. As usual before setting out on an expedition, they celebrated by downing goblets of raw Jamaican rum and firing cannon. A grand time was being had by all when suddenly—we'll never know how or why—there was a blinding flash followed by a roar. *Oxford* blew up, killing her whole three hundred fifty-man crew. Still the Morgan luck held—was, in fact, contagious. He and the officers seated on his side of the table were flung through the stern cabin windows, swimming to safety through flaming wreckage and dead bodies.

A reduced force of five hundred men in eight ships sailed for the Spanish Main a week later. The fleet's destination was Maracaibo, Venezuela, which L'Olonnois had plundered two years earlier, but which was still supposed to have much worth stealing.

A close call. Morgan's flagship, Oxford, *blows up during a drinking party off Cow Island. Only the admiral and the officers nearest to him survived by being blown through the high stern windows.*

The city lay on the western shore of an enormous freshwater lake that joined the sea by means of a narrow channel. At the lake end of the channel was a tiny island: Watch Island. L'Olonnois had easily forced his way past the island's poorly defended watchtower. The Spaniards, having learned their lesson the hard way, built a strong castle on the mainland opposite the island. Morgan's guide, a Frenchman who had been with L'Olonnois, knew nothing of this added obstacle.

One moonless night the buccaneer fleet lowered sail and drifted past Watch Island on the incoming tide, dropping anchor at the base of a tall cliff. Dawn brought them a nasty surprise: perched on the cliff above them was the castle. After an all-day battle in which both sides suffered, Morgan tried his favorite tactic of a surprise night attack.

The buccaneer chief nearly outsmarted himself this time. At the signal, his men burst into the castle and ran into a wall of—silence. The place was deserted except for some pack mules and piles of supplies. Not a Spanish soldier was to be seen anywhere.

Cheers rose from the ferocious fighters. The Spanish cowards had sneaked away rather than fight real men, they said. The rest of the expedition would be a picnic.

Morgan wasn't so sure. They had taken the castle too easily. No, they had been *given* the castle. Why?

The answer came to his nostrils in the form of a wisp of bitter-smelling smoke. Gunpowder! Gunpowder was burning somewhere nearby.

Morgan followed the odor and, sure enough, found a slow-burning fuse connected to the castle's magazine. The Spanish commander was a tricky fellow. He had turned the castle into a huge bomb set to go off when the buccaneers crowded into the main courtyard. Hastily Morgan stamped out the fuse and ordered the fleet to push on to Maracaibo. What he forgot to do was blow up the castle when he left, a mistake he would regret.

Again the buccaneers were met by silence. Maracaibo was a ghost town, deserted by all except some sick people who couldn't be moved. Everyone else had fled to the jungle with their valuables when news came that the sea rovers were back.

But Morgan would give them no peace even in the wilderness. Search parties combed the countryside for the fugitives. During the next three weeks they returned with bedraggled men and women, who were locked in churches to wait their turn with the torturers. At last, when Maracaibo seemed picked clean, Morgan sent a few prisoners ahead to Gibraltar to warn that everyone there would be tortured and killed unless the town's riches were given up without a fight. Again the frightened people fled to the jungle. And again—this time for five weeks—Morgan's bully-boys searched for prisoners, tortured, and looted. When his ships could hold no more loot or prisoners for ransom, the fleet weighed anchor and set a course for Port Royal.

In the meantime the Spaniards had been making their own plans. While the buccaneers were busy at Maracaibo and Gibraltar, three large galleons took up positions where the lake entered the channel to the sea. Worse, soldiers reoccupied the castle Morgan had failed to destroy, placing heavy cannon along its walls. The buccaneers were trapped, their small boats and guns no match for the enemy's firepower.

Not that the Spanish admiral, Don Alonso del Campo, wanted a battle if one could be avoided. A brave though cautious man, del Campo knew Morgan's knack for pulling a winning trick out of his hat at the last moment. The Spaniard thought it better to make a deal, to settle for something less than total victory, than to risk losing everything in a battle.

Del Campo gave Morgan his terms in a letter dated April 24, 1669. "My intent," he wrote, "is to dispute with you your passage out of the lake, and follow and pursue you everywhere. But if you be contented to surrender all you have taken, together with the slaves and all other prisoners, I will let you freely pass without trouble on condition that you return home to your own country." Morgan had six days to make up his mind. If at the end of that time he still couldn't decide, or decided to fight, the Spaniard promised to execute every buccaneer. "I have with me excellent soldiers who desire nothing better than to revenge on you and your people all the cruelties you have committed upon the Spanish nation in America."

Giving Morgan six days to make up his mind was the worst thing del Campo could have done, for it gave him time to think through the problem and work out a solution. Morgan gathered his men in the main square of Maracaibo to tell them they were in a tight spot. He would, he said, go along with whatever they decided in an open vote.

Did they want to escape at the cost of losing everything they had fought for during eight weeks? "No, no," they shouted.

Well, then, what did they want to do? "Fight! Fight!" the men cried, their determination growing with each outcry, which was exactly what Morgan wanted. He had a plan. He would build a *brûlot* to take care of the galleons. The word comes from the French *brûler*—to burn. A *brûlot* was a fire ship. Nothing was deadlier to a sailing vessel: not storms, not underwater obstacles, not even cannon balls. Sailing vessels were floating firetraps of wood and canvas, rope and tar. The mightiest vessels have burned to the water because a candle tipped over or someone was careless with pipe ashes.

The buccaneers approved of the plan and immediately began to prepare their fire ship. A small boat taken at Gibraltar was selected for the purpose. Sulphur, tar, gunpowder—anything that could burn and explode—was packed into the ship's hull and joined with short fuses. The timbers were loosened, extra portholes cut, so that it would break apart easily when the explosion came, showering the enemy with flame.

To make the trap as realistic as possible, logs were arranged on deck to look like cannon, each with barrels of gunpowder and a heap of cannon balls alongside. Nearby stood dummies wearing buccaneer clothing, their faces painted in, and armed with cutlass and musket. On the bridge, at the commander's post, stood a dummy with a long mustache fluffing at the ends. The only real men aboard the fire ship were twelve volunteers who would light the fuses and swim to safety as best they could.

Toward evening of the sixth day the tiny fleet set out in column formation. The fire ship led the procession, followed by Morgan's five smallest vessels with the fighting men. His three largest vessels trailed the column with the prisoners and plunder.

Dawn of May Day, 1669. Spanish lookouts sighted the buccaneers several miles away, driven ahead by a brisk land breeze. *"Pirates! Pirates! The pirates are coming!"*

Don Alonso del Campo ran from his cabin, shouting orders as he bolted up the stairs to the bridge. Instantly sails blossomed. Helmsmen strained against the great wheels as three galleons slowly turned broadside to the oncoming column. It was perfect, beautiful, an admiral's dream. Within minutes nearly one hundred big guns would be trained on the enemy's lead ships.

The men aboard the fire ship watched as the galleons grew larger. Their target was the *Magdalena*, del Campo's flagship. If she could be destroyed, there was a good chance that the others would do something stupid with their leader out of the way.

Del Campo held his fire as the lead vessel pulled ahead of the others. Surely the buccaneers didn't intend a gun duel with one small ship!

Closer and closer the ship came, del Campo holding his fire so as to make sure of its intentions. No point wasting ammunition at long range if the enemy insisted on advancing to the mouths of his cannon.

In waiting for the perfect moment to open fire, the Spaniard lost the chance to open fire at all. Before he realized what was happening, the tiny boat bumped alongside the *Magdalena*. Suddenly grapnels came flying through the air, grabbed onto its railings, and held fast.

As the Spaniards stared in horror, flames took hold of the fire ship from bow to stern. Try as they might, they couldn't push the burning vessel away or loosen its death grip. *Magdalena*'s timbers had caught fire and flames were racing up the shrouds to her sails when the fire ship shook and flew apart in a mighty explosion.

Panic seized the captains of the remaining galleons. One, thinking everything lost, ran his vessel into the shallows and sank her rather than see her captured. Morgan's five fighting ships ganged up on the third galleon, capturing her after a brief struggle.

The destruction of the Spanish squadron blocking the channel at Lake Maracaibo. As the buccaneer fleet sails ahead, the fire ship and the largest Spanish galleon burn. The guns of the castle in the distance are too far away to take part in the battle.

The buccaneers' joy didn't last long when they realized that they were still trapped. The castle atop the cliff still loomed over them as menacingly as ever. There was no way to sneak eight buccaneer vessels, plus the galleon, past the castle's guns. Trying to shoot their way out was equally suicidal.

But Morgan still had one more trick up his sleeve. It was one of the oldest tricks in the book: make the enemy think you "is where you ain't." He believed that the castle's defenders expected him to attack them next. Good. Morgan would pretend to do as they expected, then dash for freedom without firing a shot.

In broad daylight, with the Spaniards watching his every movement, Morgan sent boatloads of armed men to a wooded area behind the castle. But instead of landing, the buccaneers crouched down in the boats so that only the oarsmen could be seen returning to the ships' port sides, which faced away from the castle. Again and again boats ferried men to the shore, returning "empty," until it seemed that hundreds of men had landed.

Clearly, Morgan was up to his favorite trick of a surprise attack at night. And so the Spaniards manhandled their heavy guns from the castle's lake side to its land side. Now let the buccaneers come!

They never showed up. Under cover of night they slipped through the channel on the outgoing tide. The flabbergasted Spaniards managed to haul two or three guns back into position, but Morgan's ships were out of range before they could take aim.

Morgan stood on deck laughing. As a parting insult he fired several cannon into the night in the castle's direction, to be answered with nothing deadlier than silence.

◆◆◆

While his crews ran through their prize money at Port Royal, Morgan began to plan another operation. He hadn't forgotten his pledge to the governor of Panama at Porto Bello. More than a year had passed since then, and he was as determined as ever to keep his word. Panama City, which Drake himself hadn't dared to approach too closely, would fall under the heel of the buccaneer prince.

Panama was the jewel of New World cities. Its full name told how much the Spaniards loved it: *El Muy Noble y Leal Ciudad de Panama*—The Very Noble and Very Loyal City of Panama. The city, founded in 1519, was one hundred five years old when the Dutch bought Manhattan Island from the Indians.

As the collection point for treasure from Central and South America, Panama had become one of the wealthiest cities in the world. Its cathedral and churches had crosses and statues of solid gold covered with diamonds and pearls. Two thousand houses built of fragrant cedar wood, the homes of the wealthier merchants, lined its broad avenues. Five thousand smaller houses belonged to the shopkeepers, clerks, and soldiers. On the city's outskirts were acres of holding pens for slaves.

Panama's citizens thought their city was immune to capture. One side was built along the shore of a deepwater harbor that opened onto the Pacific Ocean. Except for the *Golden Hind*, no enemy warship had ever challenged the Spaniards in their back yard. The landward side was protected by high walls which, although needing repairs, were still strong. No wonder Panamanians shrugged their shoulders at the bad news from Porto Bello and her sister cities. It was too bad, of course, but nothing really for them to worry about. Beautiful Panama always had been, and always would be, the safest place in the New World.

So strong a place would not fall to a few hundred cutthroats. Morgan sent the word and thousands of adventurers gathered at Cow Island from as far away as Plymouth Colony and Nieu Amsterdam, as Dutchmen still called New York. Morgan's promise that this would be his biggest and best venture brought them in every imaginable type of sailing craft. The admiral's galleon rode at anchor in the midst of sleek sloops and brigs, light two-masted vessels. There were also long native canoes carved from single mahogany logs and rotting old tubs so waterlogged they wallowed rather than sailed along. When all was ready, Morgan put to sea with two thousand men aboard thirty ships. Never again would a buccaneer chief command such a force. Although they didn't know it at the time, far away in Europe statesmen were meeting to decide on actions that would sweep the buccaneers from the Caribbean and out of history.

Morgan's close shave at Lake Maracaibo had taught him never to plunge into enemy territory without securing a rear base area and a line of retreat. His plan now was to advance deep into the country by boat along the Chagres River, marching overland the rest of the way to Panama City. The mouth of the Chagres was guarded by a castle, which the buccaneers took after a bloody battle on January 6, 1671. After leaving six hundred men to occupy the castle, he led the main force upstream in dozens of captured canoes.

The journey up the Chagres was more terrible than anything Englishmen had experienced in this part of the world. Drake had friendly *Cimarrons* to guide him and care for his men's needs, but the Chagres wasn't *Cimarron* country. Morgan was on his own.

The Chagres twisted, snakelike, in wide loops, forcing the buccaneers to paddle three miles in order to go one mile upstream. The yellow water was filled with weeds, which tangled the oars, making the rowers waste their energy. Alligators swarmed in the marshes along the river-banks, waiting to fill their bellies with tasty Englishmen. Bloodsucking leeches dropped onto the men's necks from overhanging branches. Mosquitoes buzzed around their faces in clouds, invading even their mouths if they tried to speak.

Yet hunger was their cruelest enemy. The buccaneers had to be well-armed for the coming battles; but since weapons are heavy and canoes small, they set out almost without any food at all. Normally this wouldn't have been a problem, for Spanish settlers raised cattle and grew crops within a mile or two of the Chagres. Morgan had counted on landing and helping himself to this food whenever necessary. Unfortunately, Spanish scouts discovered the invaders and gave the alarm. Wherever the buccaneers went, they found empty pastures and burned crops. In the distance the smoke of burning silos curled lazily into the blue sky. The buccaneers went to sleep that first night with nothing more than a pipeful of tobacco smoke and a sip of yellow water.

Things grew worse from then on, especially when they had to leave the Chagres and climb the hills that formed the backbone of the Isthmus. Each new day brought new hardships. To satisfy their growling stomachs, men ate their leather belts, keeping their pantaloons up with lengths of prickly rope. Some lucky fellows did get something to eat. Coming upon a deserted enemy camp, they found a pile of bags made of untanned leather. No matter, they ate them with an appetite. Esquemeling, who was there, tells how the meal was prepared:

> Some who never were out of their mothers' kitchens may
> ask how (they) could eat and digest those pieces of leather,
> so hard and dry? Whom I answer that, could they once
> experiment what hunger, or rather famine, is, they would
> find the way as they did. For these first sliced it in pieces,
> then they beat it between two stones and rubbed, often
> dipping it in water, to make it supple and tender. Lastly,
> they scraped off the hair, and broiled it. Being thus cooked,
> they cut it into small morsels and ate it, helping it down
> with frequent gulps of water.

And they still kept going, stumbling along groggy
with fatigue and tortured by stomach cramps. Hunger had
become starvation. Already they were eating grass and
young leaves. Stray dogs were worth their weight in gold,
as were snakes or mice roasted and eaten with a cocked
pistol in hand.

Luckily on the sixth day they found a barn filled with
unground Indian corn, or maize. For the next three days
their stomachs wrestled with the bullet-hard kernels. On
the ninth day their journey came to an end. From the crest
of a low hill they saw Panama's church steeples glistening
in the sunlight. Beyond, stretching it seemed to the ends
of the earth, was the Pacific Ocean. Below them in a small
valley grazed a herd of cattle the Spaniards had forgotten
to drive away. Shouting their happiness, the buccaneers
waded into the terrified beasts with cutlasses and knives.
That night they slept with bellies full of red meat.

Continuing their march next morning, they found the
Spaniards waiting for them on a grassy plain outside
Panama City. The enemy commanders felt sure of victory.
For their troops not only outnumbered Morgan's forces,
they were well-fed, rested, and in good spirits.

The Spaniards were an impressive sight even from the
distance. Musketeers stood in ranks three deep, a living
wall blocking the way to the city. Squadrons of cavalry
were drawn up to the right and left of the musketeers.
Each horseman carried a long sword, two pistols, and an

eight-foot spear tipped with a steel point. Grazing peacefully behind a nearby hill was the army's "secret weapon": a herd of fifteen hundred half-wild bulls guarded by Indian cowboys.

The buccaneers came forward in regular military formation with flags flying, drums beating, trumpets blaring. Moving slowly, in a solid mass, they flowed over the field like an ocean wave. Two hundred men walked briskly ahead of the main body. Sharpshooters all, their job was to drive off attackers, allowing the main body to pour its fire into the center of the enemy line.

A trumpet call sent the Spanish cavalry into action. First at a slow trot, then at a full gallop, the squadrons sped across the field. *"Viva el Rey!"* the horsemen shouted, their swords flashing in the morning sun. "Long live the king!"

The buccaneer wave halted and stood its ground. Within seconds Morgan's men could see bearded faces, red lips, and white teeth under steel helmets.

Suddenly the sharpshooters sank to one knee, aimed, and fired their muskets as a single man. Again and again, like heartless killing machines, they fired their terrible volleys.

Nearby horses whinnied in panic and pain. Riderless horses, their eyes filled with terror, ran wild. Everywhere corpses of men and horses littered the ground.

For two hours the Spanish cavalry charged. Each time the buccaneers drove them off they rallied, charged, took their losses, and rallied again. All for nothing. When more than half of these brave men were dead and the remainder exhausted or without horses, their commanders called off the attacks.

Now for the "secret weapon." The cowboys were ordered to drive the bulls around the hill and stampede them into Morgan's army. Surely, fifteen hundred bulls, each weighing at least a ton, would leave nothing behind but some buttons and bloody rags.

But buccaneers were not the sort of people to be

frightened by stampeding cattle. They calmly waited for the animals to come within range, then, just as calmly, shot them down in their tracks. Frightened animals veered away and charged in the opposite direction, toward the Spanish musketeers. "We pursued the enemy so close," Morgan later wrote, "that their retreat came to plain running."

This old print shows the various tortures used by Morgan and his men to learn where their captives hid their treasure.

The buccaneers swept into the city behind its fleeing defenders. Warehouses along the waterfront were already being looted when a terrific explosion shook the ground. Rather than allow these half-devils to enjoy Panama, the governor had ordered the ammunition magazines blown up.

The city was doomed. Fires burned for days, fed by thousands of wooden buildings. More days passed until the heaps of cinders were cool enough to touch. Then the buccaneers went to work. Besides torturing prisoners to make them reveal the hiding places of their valuables, they dug through the ruins and sifted the ashes. The fire had not destroyed the precious metals, only changed them from statues and crosses into formless lumps. But gold is gold whatever its shape.

Morgan left the ruins three weeks later, February 14, 1671. The loot was so great that one hundred seventy-five mules were needed to carry it away. Along with the caravan came hundreds of prisoners who Morgan intended to sell into slavery in Jamaica if their relatives didn't pay ransom. When some of the women begged him to set them free, he replied that he hadn't come so far to hear weeping or see tears, "but to seek money; therefore they ought to seek that out."

Panama la Vieja—Old Panama—never rose again. The city was moved to its present location a few miles to the west, and only piles of rubble remain as a memorial to the glorious past.

Many buccaneers were dissatisfied at the way Morgan divided the loot. They had suffered too much and fought too hard to receive such small shares—only four hundred pieces of eight per man. Morgan, they complained, had kept the bulk of the treasure for himself. He had, and one night the buccaneer prince deserted his men, sneaking away with the best part of the treasure stowed aboard his flagship.

Morgan didn't care what they thought of him now, for he knew that the days of large-scale buccaneering were

An engraving of another Howard Pyle painting shows Henry Morgan's pirates and their loot after the sacking of Panama.

coming to an end. He had learned that Spain had signed a treaty recognizing Great Britain's claim to Jamaica in return for a promise to stamp out buccaneering. More importantly, Jamaica itself had grown since the rough early days. Its plantation owners and merchants were coming to believe that buccaneering hurt honest businessmen.

When news of Panama's destruction reached Spain, the government demanded that the British live up to their treaty. Morgan and his partner, Governor Modyford, were arrested and sent home for trial. Yet it was all a game to satisfy the Spaniards. Morgan was a national hero whom no jury would find guilty of "crimes" most Englishmen would have gladly copied. Instead, when the hubbub quieted down, King Charles II rewarded him with a knighthood and a new job: Lieutenant-Governor of Jamaica.

His Majesty believed in the old proverb "Set a thief to catch a thief." Peace meant an end to letters of marque and reprisal against Spain. From then on, any buccaneer who continued his attacks became a pirate in the eyes of English law. What better way to keep these fierce warriors in line than by turning their greatest leader into a policeman?

Sir Henry Morgan, buccaneer prince, became Sir Henry Morgan, champion of justice. He gave his new task all the energy he used to give to sacking Spanish cities. Many a stubborn buccaneer ended on the gallows because of "dear old Henry." Morgan was all generosity and fine words toward those who cursed him as a traitor. "God forgive 'em; I do," he said solemnly.

Morgan died peacefully in bed on August 25, 1688, at the age of fifty-three. As ships fired their guns in salute, he was buried with all the honors due Jamaica's leading citizen. At last the terror of the Spanish Main lay beneath the hot sands at the tip of the Palisadoes.

But he would not lie still for long. Less than four years later, in June 1692, an earthquake struck Port Royal. The earth shook and cracked and the waterfront slid beneath the sea. Washed away also was Sir Henry Morgan's body, and with it the grand days of Caribbean buccaneering. A new day was dawning, the day of the pirate.

IV

The Golden Age of Piracy

An old folktale tells of a pirate crew that barged through the pearly gates of heaven. Rough, evil-smelling fellows, they disturbed the heavenly peace with loud cursing and drunken singing. They would have stayed forever if Saint Peter hadn't found a way to trick them into leaving.

Standing at the entrance to heaven, the white-bearded saint pointed outside. "A ship! A ship!" he cried in great excitement.

"Where? Where?" the pirates shouted, their eyes darting back and forth.

"North-by-northwest, just over the horizon," replied the saint.

"After it!" cried the pirates as they charged through the pearly gates, which clanged shut behind them.

This story explains in its own clever way what happened to the buccaneers in the years following England's peace treaty with Spain. Many returned to cattle hunting or settled down to respectable lives as small traders and farmers. The government made it easy for them to "go straight" by offering money and land to anyone who promised to give up sea roving.

Yet there were hundreds of others who found that

peace, like war, has its problems. For them, the way of life learned during years of fighting could not be unlearned just because statesmen in Europe signed a treaty. The sea roving life, with all its dangers and hardships, drew them back with overpowering force. For where there was danger there was also adventure; hardship also meant companionship and the hope of wealth. No longer licensed to attack Spanish shipping, they became pirates, preying upon the shipping of all nations.

Peace not only made pirates of buccaneers, it scattered them to the four winds. Once England and Spain decided to stamp out buccaneering, they sent fast coast guard vessels to patrol the Greater Antilles. Before long the Brethren of the Coast found their favorite coasts too dangerous. Port Royal, Tortuga, the Cow Island anchorage and their other haunts were closed to them.

But the New World is very large and the buccaneers soon found safe harbors elsewhere. The Moskito Coast of Nicaragua had many unmapped inlets and harbors where a pirate vessel could hide or make repairs. There was also New Providence Island, one of the Bahamas group, lying at the head of the Florida Channel. New Providence was a perfect base for attacking Europe-bound ships as they passed from the Caribbean into the Atlantic.

Yet their best hideout, and safest, was in the open for everyone to see. By the late 1690s, British colonies had spread along the Atlantic coast of North America from Massachusetts to the Carolinas. These colonies were supposed to exist not for the good of their own people, but for the benefit of the mother country. Parliament had passed the Navigation Acts making it illegal for any nation except England to sell manufactured goods in the colonies, or for Americans to make these things for themselves. English merchants took advantage of their monopoly, charging the highest prices for goods that were often of the poorest quality. The Navigation Acts became one of the main causes of the American Revolution nearly a century later.

In the meantime the colonists protested by welcoming the sea rovers with open arms. Pirates were not seen as lawbreakers, but as useful people who helped the community obtain needed products at fair prices. Pirates knew that as long as they behaved themselves in port, they could roam about freely, buy supplies, and sell their loot with no questions asked.

All the leading colonial seaports—New York, Boston, Philadelphia, Charleston, Newport—did business with the pirates and grew wealthy on their ill-gotten gains. Respected colonial merchants were dealers in stolen property. The fortunes of the New Yorkers Stephen Delancey, Stephanus van Cortlandt, and Frederick Philipse were built upon profits from the "sweet trade," as pirates called their activities.

Even the King's officials had their fingers in the pirate pie. It was easy for them to smooth the way whenever a pirate captain wanted to land stolen cargo under the eyes of the customs inspectors. Easy, that is, in exchange for a pocketful of gold coins and a few uncut diamonds. Colonel Benjamin Fletcher, Royal Governor of New York in the 1690s, sold protection to any pirate who'd pay his price.

The pirates' numbers increased with time and help from men like Governor Fletcher. Ex-buccaneers were joined by unemployed privateers from Atlantic coast ports, deserters from the Royal Navy, and drifters from everywhere. Among these drifters were many blacks, who seem to have been treated as equals by their shipmates. As much as one-sixth of some pirate crews were made up of escaped slaves.

Pirates ran their vessels as the buccaneers had done before them. Crews elected their captains and signed a set of articles, or rules, before setting sail. Most pirate articles have disappeared, destroyed at the end of a voyage or thrown overboard when the ship was in danger of capture. A few sets, though, have survived. Here are the articles of the *Revenge*, Captain John Phillips, 1723:

I. Every man shall obey civil command; the Captain shall have one full share and a half in all prizes; the [sailing] master, carpenter, boatswain and gunner shall have one share and a quarter.

II. If any man shall offer to run away or keep any secret from the company, he shall be marooned, with one bottle of Powder, one bottle of water, one small arm [a pistol], and shot [bullets].

III. If any man shall steal anything in the company . . . he shall be marooned or shot. . . .

V. The man that shall strike another whilst these articles are in force shall receive Moses's Law [that is, whipped with the cat-o'-nine-tails] on the bare back.

VI. That man that shall snap his arms [that is, pull the trigger of his pistol so that the hammer strikes the flint, causing sparks], or smoke tobacco in the hold without a cap to his pipe, or carry a candle lighted without a lantern, shall suffer the same punishment as the former article.

VII. That man that shall not keep his arms clean, fit for an engagement, or neglect his business, shall be cut off from his share, and suffer such other punishment as the captain and the company shall think fit.

VIII. If any man shall lose a joint [that is, part of a limb] in time of an engagement, he shall have 400 pieces-of-eight; if a limb, 800.

Notice how strict the articles are about stealing and fighting aboard ship. A pirate crew had to be a team, which would break up if personal arguments were allowed to get out of hand. Notice also Article VI, about the use of fire belowdecks. There was almost no chance to survive if a stray spark caused a fire when the ship was on the high seas. Even if men lived through the fire, they would die of starvation and exposure drifting in row boats in the middle of the ocean. Chances of being seen and rescued by another ship were very poor.

Crews had to stick together, for the law was harsh when it caught up to seagoing bandits. Executions always took place in public as a form of entertainment and as a warning. An execution day used to be a time of festival, when people ate picnic lunches, listened to traveling musicians, and cheered as criminals were sent out of this world. Mothers brought young children to executions; that way they'd always remember what happened to lawbreakers.

Pirates in ancient times were beheaded, crucified, thrown to wild animals, and roasted alive over grills. From the 1500s onward, they were hung on a beach at low tide in such a way that their toes barely touched the water. Their bodies were then cut down and chained to a post to allow the tide to rise and fall over them three times. The remains were finally buried face down in the mud below the high water mark, where the tides quickly erased all trace of their existence.

Given such penalties, it was not a good idea for anyone taking up the sweet trade to be known by his real name. Pirates usually gave themselves nicknames or were named by their shipmates. Some captains were best known by their nicknames: "Red Hand," "Blackbeard," "Calico Jack," "Long Ben," "Gentleman Harry," "Alexander the Great," "Captain Flogger." "Half-Bottom" won his name after a cannon ball passed too close to the seat of his pants.

◆·◆

Better policing of the Caribbean drove the pirates further afield in search of prey. During the 1690s they discovered a hunting ground to satisfy the greediest of sea rovers. The Great Mogul of India ruled a Muslim empire as rich as the Spanish Main in its best days. At regular times during the year, Mogul fleets set out across the Indian Ocean from the Malabar Coast, that is, the west coast of India south of Bombay. The huge, slow-moving ships were crammed with precious goods such as spices, silks, rubies, diamonds, ivory, pearls, and cloths of gold and silver. They sailed through the Gulf of Aden into the Red Sea—red because of the coral formations that could be seen through the clear water. At ports along the way, the cargoes were transferred to camels for the trip across the desert to the Arab lands bordering the Mediterranean Sea. After completing their business, the fleets returned to India by way of the Red Sea port of Mocha with wooden chests full of gold coins.

The Great Mogul's ships shared the Indian Ocean with those of other nations. The British East India Company had trading posts known as "factories" at key points along the Malabar Coast. A steady stream of East Indiamen, seven hundred-ton vessels one hundred sixty feet long by thirty-five feet wide, carried Eastern goods to their home ports. So did Portuguese vessels from Goa and Dutch ships from the Spice Islands, as Indonesia used to be called.

Arab pirates had roamed the Indian Ocean and Red Sea for centuries, robbing pilgrims bound for the holy city of Mecca. Although a terror to the weak, they were never a problem for Mogul or European vessels. Arab dhows are tublike sailing boats and no match for big ships carrying guns.

A new breed of pirate, who stormed into the eastern seas in the 1690s, was more than a match for them. Known as the Red Sea men, they specialized in raids thousands of miles from their bases in North America.

Captain Thomas Tew, or Twoo, blazed the trail for the Red Sea men. A native of Newport, Rhode Island, Tew grew up around ships and the sea. By 1692, he was a privateer with wide experience in Caribbean and Atlantic waters. That year found him in Bermuda, where he persuaded the governor to issue letters of marque and reprisal against the French, with whom England was then at war. His license left no room for error: the seventy-ton *Amity* and its sixty-man crew were to capture French trading posts on the west coast of Africa.

Tew never had any intention of living up to his commission; it was only his excuse for piracy. *Amity* had been at sea only a few days when he told the crew that Africa was a poor place to seek one's fortune. The Red Sea! That's where a brave fellow could take a fortune overnight. At these words the crew cheered, shouting "A gold chain, or a wooden leg, we'll stand by you!"

For many weeks *Amity* glided southward along the African coast. Always the white beachline backed by the green jungle appeared on the left, the setting sun on the right. When both the beach and the setting sun were on the left, they knew they had rounded the Cape of Good Hope at the continent's tip. After that, they followed the shoreline until great patches of red began to slip under the ship's bow.

Tew had beginner's luck. *Amity* had been prowling the Red Sea for only a week when lookouts sighted a large ship with billowing sails. This vessel belonged to the Great Mogul himself and was heading for Mocha with a rich cargo.

Although the ship was well-armed and had three hundred soldiers aboard, they were not eager to die for someone else's profit. Swift little *Amity* easily overtook the lumbering vessel and, after a short fight in which the pirates lost not a single man, she surrendered. Tew had hit the jackpot, more gold and valuables than could be counted in a whole day.

Tew cruised the area for several months, hoping for another such prize. He took some ships, including an English slaver with two hundred forty Negro men, women, and children chained belowdecks. Tew knocked off their chains himself and set them free on the island of Madagascar. Unable to find anything else worth taking, he headed home, arriving at Newport in April of 1694.

What stories swept the dockside taverns! How tongues wagged, not in spite but in envy! Tew had kept his word. Each member of *Amity*'s crew landed with gold and jewels valued at three thousand pounds sterling, British money worth about three hundred and seventy-five thousand dollars today. The captain's share was said to be ten thousand pounds, worth at least a million dollars in buying power today.

Pirate Tew became Gentleman Tew overnight. The wealthiest Newport families invited the captain, his wife,

The first of the Red Sea men. Captain Tew smokes his long clay pipe while telling of his adventures to his friend, Governor Fletcher of New York. A painting by Howard Pyle.

and two daughters to their homes. The women arrived dressed in fine silks—all stolen. Their costumes were completed by diamond earrings, gold and diamond necklaces, and heavy gold bracelets—all stolen too.

Nothing was too good for Captain Tew. Governor Fletcher invited him to dinner in his New York mansion. When complaints reached London that His Excellency was too chummy with pirates, he had no idea, he explained, that Tew was a lawbreaker. He lied. He also said that he invited Tew because "I wished in my mind to make him a sober man, and in particular to cure him of the vile habit of swearing." He lied again. What Governor Fletcher really wanted was gifts and a chance to do business with the lucky pirate.

Tew might have lived to a ripe old age if greed and the itch for adventure hadn't gotten the best of him. After six months ashore, he began to prepare *Amity* for another voyage. When his intentions became known, young men from New York and Rhode Island fought each other for the privilege of signing his articles. Servants ran away from their masters. Poor lads left their parents and headed for the docks. Even sons of wealthy families begged for a place aboard *Amity*.

Tew's second voyage began as a carbon copy of the first. Soon after arriving in the Red Sea, September, 1695, an Indian merchantman hove into view and was attacked. No sooner did the battle begin, when it came to an end. A cannon ball struck Tew in the stomach, killing him instantly. So horrible was his death, and so terrified was his crew at the sight of his mangled body, that they surrendered. We don't know what happened to the captured pirates, but it couldn't have been anything pleasant.

◆▶

Sea rovers remembered Tew's fabulous first voyage, not his horrible end. His success triggered a kind of "gold rush" to the East. On any given day no fewer than fifteen pirate craft were to be found cruising the Indian Ocean and nearby waters.

Those who followed Tew had to work out new ways of operating far from home for long periods of time. The Indian Ocean and Red Sea were not like the Caribbean, with its friendly ports and out-of-the-way harbors where a ship could be hidden. The Red Sea men needed a base close to their hunting grounds, yet far enough away so they could have early warning of enemy warships.

Madagascar was perfect for their needs. The fourth largest island in the world,* Madagascar lies two hundred sixty miles off Africa's east coast and two thousand four hundred miles southeast of the Malabar Coast. It had good harbors, plenty of fresh water, and citrus fruits such as limes. Being rich in vitamin C, these fruits prevented scurvy, a disease that could wipe out an entire crew. British sailors are still called "limeys," or "lime-juicers," because they were made to drink a few ounces of the sour juice each morning.

Pirates built forts, or "castles," as they called them, high on Madagascar's cliffs. Surrounded by ditches and earth walls topped with sharpened tree trunks, these were strong defenses, although nothing like those of the Spanish Main. On a clear day a man with a spyglass could see fifty miles in every direction.

The pirate's castle was also his home, where he relaxed between voyages. Here the food was good and plentiful. Native cooks dished out heaping platters of boiled beef and roast pork. Deep bowls of sea-turtle soup were served piping hot and laced with sherry wine. Although nearly wiped out today, the giant sea turtle was plentiful three centuries ago.

Pirates drank well, too. Many crews swore off alcohol while at sea, but they easily made up for this sacrifice during rest periods ashore. Their favorite drinks were brandy-punch and rumfustian, a mixture of gin, beer, sherry wine, and spices. A wicked brew of rum and gunpowder left the drinker with a Madagascar-size headache when he woke up next morning.

Pirates entertained themselves as best they could. Every vessel had its "musickers"—drummers, fifers, fid-

---

* Only Greenland, New Guinea, and Borneo are larger.

The mock trial was one of the pirates' favorite ways of passing time ashore. The spectacled "judge" sits in a tree and passes out his sentences.

dlers, trumpeters—who earned extra pay for playing snappy tunes. At such times, if they were really in the mood, these roughnecks danced jigs and reels with one another.

Many hours were spent acting out mock trials in which everyone played a part: judge, jurors, defense lawyer, prosecutor, jailers, executioner. Besides passing the time, this "play" had a serious side. Each man knew what to expect if the law caught up to him: a short trial and a rope around the neck. The mock trial helped to overcome the fear of death by making it seem funny.

Capturing ships on the high seas was no laughing matter. Unlike the Caribbean, where a pirate craft could dart out at its prey from behind an island, there were no hiding places on the Indian Ocean. The slowest East Indiaman could outrun the fastest pirate craft given a fair wind and a lead of twenty miles.

Yet how could a captain know whether or not a distant craft belonged to pirates? Ships at sea didn't automatically crowd on sail and flee the moment they saw each other. The oceans are wide, voyages long and lonely. Seamen had a natural curiosity about any vessel they met. It was good to hail another ship, to exchange news and fill in provisions. The trouble came when you realized that curiosity had brought you within range of pirates.

Pirates were masters of trickery, of hiding their intentions until it was too late. Since they carried flags of all nations, they could calm suspicions by hoisting the colors of the ship they wanted to capture. Some pirates went so far as dressing a few shipmates as women who'd wave and call to the other ship to come closer.

The captain who took this bait soon regretted his foolishness. As the distance between the two vessels closed, his nation's flag suddenly slid down the rope line and its place was taken by a red banner, or "Red Jack."

Pirate ships used flags of two colors to signal their intentions. All seamen knew that a red banner was a call to surrender peacefully and a promise that they would not be harmed. But if the merchant captain decided to fight, the Red Jack was hauled down. In its place the Black Flag, the Jolly Roger, snapped in the breeze.

The word "Roger" is English slang for "rogue"—a wanderer, vagabond, rover. During the 1600s each pirate captain designed his own personal Jolly Roger flag. Black in color, these flags were decorated with various symbols for death such as skeletons, skulls, crossed bones, spears,

Bartholomew Roberts

Jack Rackam

Henry Avery

Walter Kennedy

Emanuel Wynne

Blackbeard

Thomas Tew

Stede Bonnet

A selection of Jolly Roger flags. Each pirate captain designed his own Jolly Roger, or Black Flag, which he used to warn crews of merchant ships that they'd be killed if they didn't surrender without a fight.

hourglasses, cutlasses. Thomas Tew's flag, for example, showed an arm swinging a cutlass. "Long Ben" Avery preferred a skull set above two crossed leg bones. Captain Bartholomew Roberts' flag showed himself and a spear-carrying skeleton holding an hourglass, the sign that time had run out. It had, because raising the Jolly Roger meant that no prisoners would be taken. It was a battle to the death.

The merchant captain used the little time he had left to prepare a defense. Merchant ships were not men-of-war, pure fighting vessels. Ordinary seamen had to fight professional killers. It was not a task they liked.

Pikes, grenades, and cutlasses were brought up from the magazine and given out. Swivel guns were set up; these were tiny cannon mounted on the deck railings with a turning attachment to allow them to be aimed by one man. Known as "murdering pieces," swivel guns fired chunks of scrap iron.

The captain knew that his men were terrified of the Jolly Roger and would desert if they had the chance. His job was to keep them at their posts no matter what happened. Ladders to the lower decks were taken away to prevent their running below. Generous portions of "liquid courage"—beer, brandy, rum, wine—were issued. Crews often fought for their lives drunk and bleary-eyed. The musickers blared, squeaked, and rapped out warlike tunes.

The pirates tried to come alongside the merchantmen and bind it with grapnels or deliberately crash into its bow. Boarders then scrambled over the rails and ran along the bowsprit like tightrope walkers. Unlike movie pirates, real pirates tried not to fire cannon into the hull of their victim ship for fear it would sink before they could take off its cargo.

No mercy was shown to the crew that resisted and lost the battle. Men were stabbed, shot, or tied up and thrown overboard. Some were "sweated," made to run in circles around the mast as pirates jabbed them with cutlasses and broken bottles. There is, however, no truth to the legend about prisoners being blindfolded and made to "walk the plank" into the sea with their hands tied. Never once in all the reported cases of piracy did such a happening take place.

———◆◆◆———

Next to Captain Tew, Henry Avery was the most famous Red Sea man. "Long Ben," as everyone called him because he was a tall fellow, was born about 1665, near Plymouth, England. As so often happened with poor boys, he went to sea early in order not to be a burden to his parents. After gaining experience aboard slave ships, he became first mate of the *Duke*, a forty-six-gun privateer hired by the Spaniards to fight French pirates in the Caribbean.

But Long Ben had other plans. He had listened open-mouthed to stories of treasure waiting to be taken in the east by daring men. *He* was a daring man, and determined to have his share.

May, 1694, found *Duke* riding at anchor in the harbor of La Coruña, Spain, waiting for orders to cross the Atlantic. Avery had already persuaded most of the crew to mutiny and was waiting for the right moment to take over the vessel. His chance came one night when the captain passed out after having too much to drink. As he lay on his bunk fast asleep, Avery's mutineers locked the loyal seamen below and sailed quietly out of the harbor.

Duke had been at sea many hours when her captain began to stir. Something in his alcohol-soaked brain alerted him to unusual sounds, sounds an anchored ship shouldn't be making. Cables creaked, while the vessel rose and fell rhythmically in the ocean's swells. The captain rubbed the sleep from his eyes and rang his bell for First Mate Avery.

"What is the matter?" he asked.

"Nothing," the pirate answered.

Not satisfied, the captain asked in a loud voice, "Something's the matter with the ship? What weather is it?"

"No, no," Avery explained. "Don't be in a fright, but

"Long Ben" Avery poses in front of a battle scene. The pirate outsmarted himself by trying to sell stolen diamonds to English merchants who were even better thieves than himself.

put on your clothes and I'll let you in on a secret. You must know that I am captain of this ship now, and this is my cabin, and therefore you must walk out."

The terrified captain was given two choices: he could sail under the Jolly Roger, if he gave up drinking, or be set free. The captain and a few others asked to be put ashore in the ship's longboat.

Avery arrived at the entrance to the Red Sea in August, 1695, where he met and joined forces with two other pirate craft. At first the tiny wolf pack had bad luck. A twenty-five-ship convoy was sighted, but the admiral gave them the slip during the night.

Their disappointment was forgotten with the morning's first light. For nearby, making way slowly under full sail, was the largest ship most of Avery's men had ever seen. The *Gunsway*, as she was called, belonged to none other than the Great Mogul. Besides the usual cargo of valuables, she carried six hundred pilgrims bound for the Muslim holy places at Mecca.

The pirates easily headed off the lumbering vessel and a cannon duel began at a distance of a hundred yards. *Gunsway*'s gunners were holding their own when tragedy struck. One of their own cannon exploded, flinging chunks of red-hot iron around the gun deck. Some well-aimed shots by Avery's gunners, meanwhile, brought down her mainmast. The rest was only a matter of boarding and swordplay.

Gunsway's cargo holds were brimming with precious things, including jewels and one hundred thousand pieces of eight and an equal number of "sequins," Arab gold coins. In an unusual show of kindness, Avery allowed the vessel to go its way without murdering the crew and passengers. Maybe he was so happy with the loot that he felt generous toward these unfortunates.

Long Ben certainly showed no generosity toward his fellow pirates. As they sailed toward Madagascar, he persuaded the captains of the other two vessels that it would be safer to leave their share of the loot with him. His ship was fastest and had the best chance of escaping if they ran into trouble. The other captains agreed to his plan. The three ships kept company for three days and nights. On the morning of the fourth day, there were only two.

Avery arrived at New Providence in the Bahamas two months later. Governor Nicholas Trott, as great a rascal as you could find in the Americas, welcomed the pirates. He could afford to be nice, since Avery's men had to hand over thousands of dollars in gold and ivory for the privilege of landing. The one thing the governor couldn't sell them was a pardon for their crimes.

Avery's crew decided to split up, each man going his own way with his share of the loot. Several headed for the American colonies, where they vanished from history. One lucky sailor married the daughter of Governor Markham of Pennsylvania, who gladly offered pirates protection for a price.

The other crewmen bought small boats and sailed for Ireland and England, where they quickly aroused suspicion. Sailors were supposed to be too poor to pay shopkeepers with Arab sequins. Lawmen began to ask questions. One by one Avery's men were searched and arrested when they couldn't explain how they had come by such wealth.

The chief thief—Avery—settled in a seacoast town near Plymouth. He was set for life, he thought. From now on he expected to live quietly as a prosperous gentleman. He didn't.

Long Ben Avery soon discovered that he had outsmarted himself. He had chosen to take his share of *Gunsway*'s treasure not in gold, but in dozens of diamonds. These sparkling beauties proved to be his undoing. Like any burglar today, Avery found that he had to turn his loot into cash, otherwise it was worthless.

The pirate sent word to some merchants in the city of Bristol that he had valuable "goods" to sell, but wanted to sell quietly, without fuss. As it turned out, these merchants were smarter thieves than the master pirate. He stole at the point of the sword; they stole with soft words and friendly smiles.

The Bristol men visited Avery, examined the diamonds, and swore they were worth a king's ransom. They'd love to buy them, they said, but didn't have the cash for such a large deal. Would Avery allow them to take the diamonds to show to wealthy customers in the city? In the meantime, they'd leave him some money to live on. Avery agreed. They walked out. He never saw them again.

Months passed, and Avery's money ran out. He wrote letter after letter to Bristol to demand the money owed him or the diamonds' return. Neither arrived. The thieving merchants had him where they wanted. What could he do? Sue them in court? Call the police?

Long Ben Avery, retired pirate, never got over his loss. He died a pauper, unable to afford even a plain coffin. It is said that he cursed the merchants with his dying breath for being "as good pirates at land as he was at sea."

—————◆•◆—————

The Red Sea men had scared the British East India Company out of its wits. Every packet of messages brought news of the loss of more precious cargo. Profits tumbled. And, worst of all, the Great Mogul threatened to close company's factories unless the English pirates were brought under control.

The East India Company turned to the government, begging for a squadron of warships to patrol the Eastern Seas. The request was turned down, because the Royal Navy had enough to do fighting the French without chasing pirates on the other side of the world. The only help the British Government could send was a fifty-year-old sea captain named William Kidd.

—————◆•◆—————

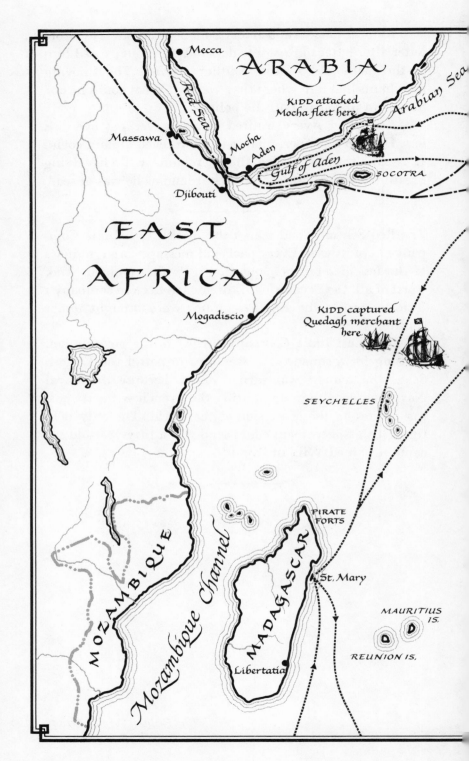

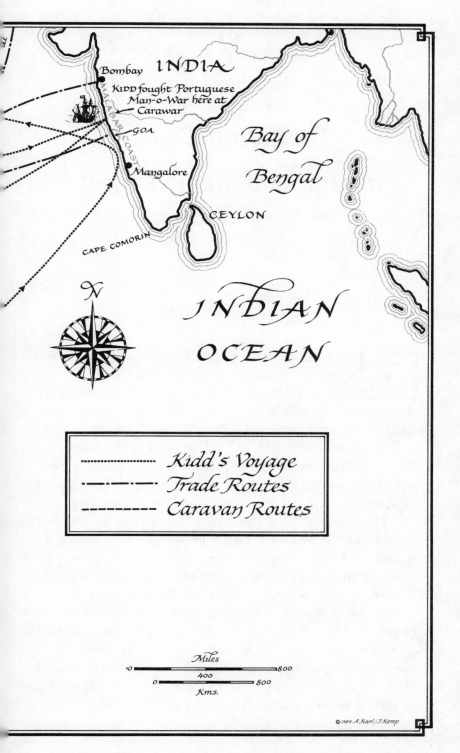

A Map of Captain Kidd's Adventures in the Adventure Galley.

V

The Devil's Twins:
Captain Kidd and Blackbeard

T wo centuries ago, Captain Kidd and piracy were spoken of in the same breath. Kidd was the most famous pirate of all time. Mothers sent naughty children to bed with warnings that the sea-roving monster would steal them if they didn't behave. American folklore is rich in tales of Kidd's buried treasure and of treasure hunters chased by his ghost with a raised cutlass. People still search lonely stretches of coast, hoping to unearth his "lost treasure." They never have, and never will, succeed.

How strange it is, then, that the terrible Kidd never thought of himself as a pirate or sailed under the Jolly Roger. Until the hangman's noose silenced him forever, he swore he was an honest man wrongly condemned to death.

William Kidd was born about 1645 in the port city of Greenock, Scotland. The son of a Protestant minister, he received a good education before going to sea as a teenager. The sea treated him kindly at first. He rose to the command of privateer vessels in the Caribbean and used his earnings to start his own business. In the early 1690s, he settled in New York City, where he lived happily with his wife and two children. He owned a fine house, several trading vessels, and enjoyed the respect of his neighbors. Everyone thought him honest and hardworking, and there is nothing to prove that they were wrong. An old pew in Trinity Church in Wall Street has a brass plate with the inscription: *"Captain William Kidd."*

The doings of the Red Sea men ended this comfortable way of life. It all happened in an unexpected way. During the summer of 1695, King William III decided to stamp out piracy. He began by replacing Governor Fletcher with the Earl of Bellomont, a stern nobleman noted for his honesty. As governor of both New York and New England, Bellomont had the authority to move against the pirates and their friends in any way he thought necessary.

It so happened that Kidd, who was in London at the time on business, was introduced to the new governor. His Lordship greeted him with an idea that must have set his head spinning. Bellomont and some other noblemen wanted to outfit a vessel capable of tracking down the Red Sea men in their own hunting grounds. Since it was to be a private expedition, and expensive as well, its backers and the ship's captain would share both the costs and profits. Whenever a pirate vessel was taken, any treasure found aboard was to be sold and the money shared by the backers, captain, and crew.

Now came the clincher: he, Captain Kidd, had been chosen to lead the expedition. If he refused the "honor," it would be taken as a sign of disloyalty to the king. And such a person, Bellomont added, could not be allowed to do business in New York colony.

His lordship had made Captain Kidd an offer he couldn't refuse. In return, Bellomont obtained a commission from King William authorizing "our trusty and well-beloved, Captain Kidd," to capture Thomas Tew (whose death had not yet been reported) and any other Englishmen turned pirate. He also obtained letters of marque and reprisal against the French, which, everyone thought, would guarantee the voyage's success.

Kidd's ship, the *Adventure Galley*, was launched during the winter. At first glance she seemed to be a perfect pirate-chaser. Sleek and trimlined, she weighed in at two hundred eighty seven tons and carried thirty-four cannon. Yet she had been cheaply built, which meant that Kidd had to accomplish his mission quickly or risk the vessel's falling apart beneath his feet.

Finding a crew also gave Kidd no end of trouble. It was important to have men who were not only good sailors and fighters, but who would not join the pirates at the first opportunity. It was always difficult to find such men; doubly difficult since the Royal Navy needed them for its warships. Kidd managed to find only seventy good men. He intended to bring *Adventure Galley* up to fighting strength by signing on another ninety men in New York.

Things began to go wrong from the moment he set sail in February, 1696. As *Adventure Galley* glided down the Thames River toward the English Channel, she was stopped by a man-of-war. An officer came aboard with a squad of marines and "pressed" most of Kidd's best men. Pressing, or impressing, was the Royal Navy's right to board any English vessel and take against his will any seaman needed to fill gaps in a warship's crew. When Kidd protested and showed the royal commission, the man-of-war's captain sent him an equal number of replacements—his worst men, most of whom knew their way around His Majesty's jails. Arriving in New York, Kidd could find only more men of this type. At last, after months of delay, *Adventure Galley* left for the East in September, 1696.

Kidd was shocked at what he *didn't* find when he arrived at his destination. No pirates were to be seen anywhere. Not in their haunts in Madagascar. Not in the Indian Ocean or along the Malabar Coast. Not in the Red Sea. Kidd was missing them at every turn. Wherever he went, they had left a few days earlier. The only ships seen were flying friendly colors, not the Jolly Roger.

Weeks melted into months without sighting a prize. Food and supplies began to run short. The sails drooped as the wind died down and the sun baked the men's backs a deep bronze. Everyone was miserable.

The crew began to grumble. They had signed Kidd's articles under the old buccaneer rule of "no prey, no pay." Over a year had passed since they last saw home or earned a penny. It was all the captain's fault, they said. If he really cared about his men he'd snap up one of those fat Malabar ships cruising in the distance. Who would know? Who would care? No one would notice if some ship disappeared in the middle of nowhere.

Kidd shouted them down each time they brought up the idea of turning pirate. Privateering was one thing, piracy another. And William Kidd was no son of the Jolly Roger. A sentence from his commission held him back with an iron grip: "We do charge and command you, as you will answer the same at your utmost peril, that you do not, in any manner, offend or molest any of our friends or allies, their ships or subjects." *At your utmost peril*: these were King William's words, and disobeying them meant death.

The crew grew angrier as he let richly laden Indian ships pass in safety. Mutiny hung in the air like a storm cloud. A Drake or a Morgan would have known how to deal with such disloyalty. But Kidd, although a good seaman, was a poor leader when the going became rough.

The storm burst several days after Kidd allowed an especially rich prize to get away. He was pacing the deck when he saw William Moore, the chief gunner, sharpening a chisel. They began to argue, Moore accusing the captain of turning the crew into beggars.

"You lousy dog!" Kidd shouted, his face flushed, the veins in his neck bulging.

"If I am a lousy dog, you have made me so," Moore shot back. "You have brought me to ruin, and many more."

Kidd lost control of himself. Suddenly he caught a heavy wooden bucket by its strap and smashed it into Moore's head with all his might. The gunner went down in a pool of blood and died the next day of a fractured

Captain Kidd loses his temper and kills his chief gunner, William Moore, with an iron-bound bucket. Moore had insulted him for not attacking richly laden merchantmen in the Indian Ocean.

skull. "Damn him, he is a villain," was the captain's only comment.

Yet in death, Moore had won. For Kidd now decided that his "utmost peril" lay here, aboard *Adventure Galley*, not half a world away in London. He decided the crew would murder him any day unless he took some prizes.

Kidd noted that whenever he neared a strange vessel, it raised a British flag; and if he boarded it the captain showed him an English pass. Passes were official letters guaranteeing safe conduct in case a vessel was stopped by privateers of the nation issuing them. Gradually it became clear to him that merchantmen were as good as playing tricks with flags as pirates. Each vessel had a set of flags and passes which it showed whenever necessary.

Kidd decided to trick the tricksters. The next time he saw an Indian ship, he hoisted *French* colors. Sure enough, its captain raised a French flag and showed a French pass when boarded. "By God, I have catched you!" Kidd roared.

"You are a free prize of England!" After that, he was able to capture one ship after another using the same trick. Most vessels were small fry with little valuable cargo, but worth taking to satisfy his rebellious crew.

Early in February 1698, Captain Kidd captured a gorgeous prize. She was the *Quedah Merchant*, a five hundred-tonner carrying a cargo of silks, gold, silver, jewels, sugar, iron, and guns. The only thing French about her was her flag and pass. She belonged to an Indian, carried cargo owned by Armenians, and was skippered by an Englishman. She was definitely friendly. No matter. She had shown French colors, and England and France were enemies. That was enough, as far as Kidd was concerned.

She was a lucky catch in more than one way. By this time *Adventure Galley* was falling apart. Kidd's ship leaked so badly that the pumps had to be worked around the clock and ropes cinched around the hull to prevent the timbers from separating. Kidd arrived at Madagascar just in time to transfer his crew and loot to the *Quedah Merchant*.

Kidd also stumbled upon his long-lost pirates. A brute named Captain Culliford had put into Madagascar for repairs a few days earlier. But instead of clapping him in irons, Kidd greeted him as a long lost friend. "Before I would do you any harm," he said, "I would have my soul fry in hell."

For once Kidd's crew agreed with their captain. Ninety-seven men deserted to Culliford, taking whatever supplies they wanted from the *Quedah Merchant*. Kidd could only watch, his mouth scared shut; for they said they needed only the smallest excuse to pump him full of pistol balls.

Kidd was glad to put to sea with the remainder of his crew. After the normal five-month voyage, *Quedah Merchant* dropped anchor off Anguilla in the West Indies. Another surprise waited for him here. The shore party he sent to buy supplies came racing back with oars flashing. The islanders, they said, gasping for breath, had refused to sell them anything because their captain was a pirate. The date: April Fool's Day, 1699.

Still, *this* was no April Fool's prank. News of Kidd's adventures had set London buzzing. Again the Great Mogul made threats, and backed them up by throwing East India Company merchants into jail. Again the company's representatives begged for help. The government replied by declaring Kidd a pirate and setting a price on his head.

A stunned and worried Captain Kidd paced *Quedah Merchant*'s bridge as it threaded its way among the Lesser Antilles. He was in deep trouble, although probably not deep enough to drown him, he thought. A plan began to form in his mind. As a first step he beached the big ship along the Hispaniola coast, where he bought a smaller, faster vessel, the *Antonio*. Then the pirates sped north toward the gathering storm clouds.

The second part of Kidd's plan depended upon Lord Bellomont, who had arrived in Boston the year before. He (Kidd) could explain everything, while His Lordship could fix anything with the authorities in London. The nobleman would have to help him, for wasn't it he who had pressured him into going on this voyage in the first place?

Kidd was wrong all the way. Lord Bellomont had been deeply embarrassed by his partner's actions. Not only did His Lordship believe Kidd guilty, he felt he had to capture him to set things right with King William.

After stopping in Delaware Bay to put ashore crewmen who wanted to go their own ways, Kidd sailed to Gardiner's Island, which lies off the eastern end of Long Island near Montauk Point. Kidd left most of his loot there for safekeeping with John Gardiner, the island's owner, and sent a message to Lord Bellomont.

The shrewd nobleman set his trap carefully. Although he could not grant a pardon, he pledged, "on my word and on my honor," to do everything in his power to see that

In this old print, Captain Kidd, bound with giant chains and locks, waits in Boston's Stone Jail for the authorities to decide his fate.

Kidd got what he deserved. He meant a rope, which Kidd now rushed to put around his neck.

Kidd crowded on every inch of sail and sped to Boston. He was ashore only a few hours when the police arrested him, loaded him with chains, and locked him in Boston's Stone jail, a cold, damp dungeon. Police were sent to seize the loot stored on Gardiner's Island.

Rumors continue to this day that the Gardiner's Island treasure was only the tip of the iceberg, that Kidd had buried a huge treasure somewhere along the New York coast. He didn't, nor did anyone else.

Stories of buried pirate treasure chests, of captains shooting crewmen and tumbling their bodies into the hole so that their ghosts would guard the loot are just that— stories. A crewman might bury his share to keep it safe while he went into hiding. But loot belonging to a whole crew was never buried in one place. It was too risky, because too many people would have to share the secret. Pirates *always* divided their booty as soon as possible. Captured pirates sometimes tried to trade their "buried treasure" for their lives, but lawmen were wise to this trick and they wound up on the gallows.

Captain Kidd's own date with the hangman was drawing near. Sent to London for trial on charges of murdering Moore and of piracy, he could only put up a weak defense. The French passes, which might have helped his case, "disappeared" until the early 1900s, when they were found in a bundle of old papers in a government office. Kidd's requests for a lawyer were put off until the last moment, preventing a proper defense. He was found guilty on all charges and sentenced to die on May 23, 1701.

On that morning Kidd and other condemned men were placed in a cart and driven through the streets of London to Execution Dock on the Thames River. Crowds followed the death cart, singing and joking as if on holiday. Kidd probably didn't notice the celebration because he was drunk.

There was still one more surprise in store for William Kidd. When the hangman let him drop, the rope snapped, sending him crashing to the ground. He was dragged into place for another try, and this time the rope held.

Since Kidd was a special criminal, his body received special treatment. After the tide had risen and fallen over it three times, it was covered with tar to preserve it, wrapped in chains, and hung on a gallows along the shore,

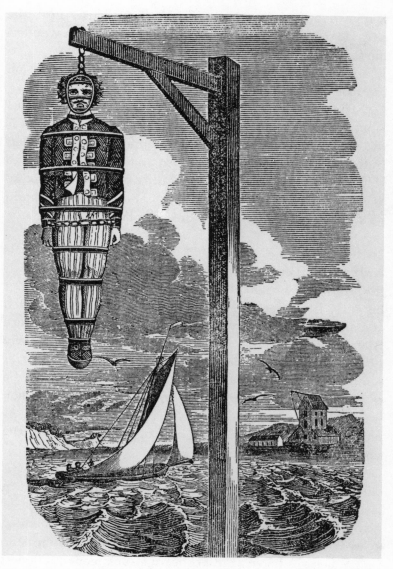

Kidd, tarred and hung in chains, swings on the gallows along the Thames River as a warning to all against taking up the "sweet trade" of piracy.

where it remained for many years as a warning to would-be pirates.

New Yorkers used to say that on dark nights, when lightning zigzagged across the sky and thunder rattled windows, a seaman came to lonely farmhouses near the city. He seemed so weary, so sad, as if he had been wandering for ages.

KNOCK. KNOCK. KNOCK. Bony fingers rapped on the door.

His clothes were heavy with water. And they smelled —not of fresh rain, but of the salty sea.

The man asked where he was and for a night's shelter. In the morning, he paid for his bed and meals with Indian gold. But his eyes were still red with weariness, his clothes as wet and salty-smelling as ever. The ghost of Captain Kidd was still searching for the way home.

———— ◆•◆ ————

Next to Captain Kidd, the most famous pirate was a bawling, brawling brute called Blackbeard. Little is known of his early life except that his real name was Edward Teach and that as a young man he settled in New Providence Island in the Bahamas, a favorite pirate base in the early 1700s. There he met Benjamin Hornigold, commander of a small but deadly pirate squadron. Hornigold taught the eager youngster everything he knew about piracy, which was indeed a great deal. And since Blackbeard was an A-plus student, Hornigold gave him his first command, the sloop *Queen Anne's Revenge.*

Blackbeard went out on his own in 1716, after his chief decided to accept the Royal Pardon and settle down to a peaceful life in the Bahamas. Scorning any idea of giving up "the sweet trade" of piracy, Blackbeard sailed away with his sloop and one other in search of a better base.

Wherever he went, Blackbeard struck fear into honest seamen. The American colonies had never seen or heard of anyone like him before. Tew, Avery, and Kidd were gentle stay-at-homes compared to this wild man. At six-feet-four-inches tall, broad-shouldered, weighing over two hundred pounds, he seemed like a walking mountain. Few people at this time reached six feet owing to poor diet during their growing years. Blackbeard was also as strong as he looked.

He could keep swinging his cutlass after most men collapsed from exhaustion. He used to add gunpowder to his rum, light it, and swallow the flaming mixture in a gulp.

Yet Blackbeard didn't depend upon strength alone to win victories. He was ahead of his time, an expert in what we call "psychological warfare." He realized that a clever person could so terrify an enemy as to have him half beaten before firing the first shot.

To see Blackbeard in action was to remember him in nightmares for the rest of your life. He deserved his nickname, for seldom has there been a beard like his. This beard, said the author Daniel Defoe, was "like a frightful Meteor, covered his whole Face, and frightened America more than any Comet that has appeared there for a long time." It was the blackest black in color and coarse as steel wool. Beginning under the eyes, it spread over the entire face, reaching down to the middle of the chest. To make it more frightening, the pirate braided it into tails, which he twisted back over his ears or tied with colorful ribbons.

Lighted gunner's matches were stuck under his hat as a final touch of terror. These, we remember, were ropes dipped in saltpeter to make them burn slowly. The bravest fighter trembled at seeing Blackbeard leap onto his deck. Fierce eyes glowered from out of a cloud of smoke, as if their owner had just been shot out of hell.

He fought like a devil, too. Completely fearless, he loved a cut-and-stab brawl across the deck of some unlucky merchantman. Besides his cutlass and a beltful of knives, he had six pistols in holsters slung across his chest. Swinging his cutlass with the right hand, from time to time he drew a pistol with the left hand. He fired pointblank into an opponent's chest or face. If he missed, he used the pistol as a club or threw it.

Even Blackbeard's sense of humor was scary. Getting bored one day, he shouted, "Come, let's make a hell of our own, and try how long we can bear it." Three men went below with him, the hatch was sealed, and large pots of sulphur were lit. Clouds of yellow, suffocating smoke filled

Blackbeard in battle dress. Armed with pistols, a sword, and a cutlass, gunners' matches smoking under his hat, he was as frightening in battle as he was brave.

their lungs, until the crewmen thought they would die. Blackbeard roared with laughter as they broke open the hatch and crawled on deck, panting, to breathe the fresh air. Then the captain came up with bulging eyes and a face pale as a dead man's.

"Why, captain," said a startled man, "you look as if you were coming straight from the gallows!"

"My lad," Blackbeard answered, "that's a brilliant idea. Next time we shall play at gallows and see who can swing longest on the string without being choked!"

Another time he invited two cronies to his cabin for a drink. As they sat around the table, he drew two pistols, blew out the candle, crossed his hands under the table, and pulled the triggers. One shot missed; the other smashed the knee of his first mate, crippling him for life. When asked why he had injured a friend, Blackbeard grinned, explaining "If I did not now and then kill one of you, you'll forget who I am." The crew put up with his pranks out of fear and because he never let a rich prize get away.

Blackbeard liked women and they liked him. They got along so well that he married at least fourteen times. There are many legends about Blackbeard and his wives. The most famous says that he amused himself by making his wife dance until she collapsed from exhaustion. The pirate sat sprawled in an easy chair, a pistol in each hand. Faster and faster she danced until, growing tired, she slowed down. But not for long, for a few well-aimed bullets near her toes sent her on her way again. Yet there is no proof that Blackbeard ever shot at his wives, or killed them when he wanted to take another bride. Why should he? It was easy enough to put an unwanted wife ashore in the next port and sail away knowing they would never meet again.

After leaving New Providence Island, Blackbeard cruised along the coast northward from Florida, capturing merchantmen as he went. Arriving off the port city of Charleston, South Carolina, he dropped anchor and waited for his prey to come to him. Within days five valuable ships had fallen into his hands. News of his blockade spread quickly, until no captain dared to sail out of or into Charleston harbor.

Blackbeard became so bold that he sent a landing party ashore to get a fresh supply of medicines and bandages. Not that he intended to *buy* what he needed; Blackbeard never bought anything he could steal. The governor of South Carolina was informed that unless the medicines were handed over soon, or if any harm came to his men, all the prisoners he took from the ships would be killed.

The governor and his council were angry and frightened. While they discussed Blackbeard's demands, his bullies swaggered around the streets as if they owned the place. Citizens peered at them from behind closed shutters, praying they would leave. Finally, the governor swallowed his pride and gave the pirates the medicines. It was shameful to pay blackmail, but what was a chest of medicines when so many innocent lives were at stake?

Satisfied at last, Blackbeard released his prisoners and continued up the coast to Bath, North Carolina. Although most colonial ports had been closed to pirates since Captain Kidd's day, they still found a welcome in North Carolina. Governor Charles Eden was bribed to say that Blackbeard had reformed and deserved a pardon. While ashore he did seem to be a model citizen, obeying the laws and spending his money freely. He wouldn't dream of robbing anyone, let alone chasing them with a cutlass.

But Bath was on dry land; things were different at sea, where he was busier than ever. No ship sailing along the coast was safe. Blackbeard stopped any ship he wanted, murdered the crew if they fought back, and sailed away free as the breeze.

South Carolina's merchants and sea captains felt angry and powerless. Appeals to Governor Eden went nowhere; he promised to take action, but never lifted a finger. As long as Blackbeard paid for protection, law-abiding citizens could whistle from the rooftops for all the governor cared.

Toward the end of 1718, they grew tired of complaining and decided to act on their own. Governor Alexander Spotswood of Virginia was known to be an honest man who hated pirates. A group of North Carolinians secretly contacted Spotswood, asking him to get rid of Blackbeard. Of course he'd help; nothing would please him more than putting an end to this pirate once and for all.

Spotswood could back up his promise with force. The Royal Navy had two warships, H.M.S. *Pearl* and H.M.S. *Lyme*, on patrol in Virginian waters. They were fine vessels, but too heavy to go after Blackbeard at Ocracoke Island, his favorite hiding place. Now part of the Cape Hatteras National Seashore, Ocracoke is a small, low-lying island surrounded by underwater sandbars crisscrossed by shallow channels. Unless you knew the way, as Blackbeard did, you'd run aground, making a perfect target for the pirate's guns.

Spotswood used his own money to hire two sloops small enough to navigate the Ocracoke shallows. Manning these vessels were fifty-eight sailors from the warships under the command of Lieutenant Robert Maynard. Blackbeard was about to meet his match.

The sloops anchored off Ocracoke Island toward evening on November 22, 1718. In the distance, at the tip of the island, behind the sandbars, they could see the masts of Blackbeard's ship. Maynard decided to wait until dawn before entering the treacherous channel.

Blackbeard meanwhile had seen the sloops, but spent the night drinking his favorite mixture of rum and gunpowder. He was not worried in the least, having been in tighter spots before. Besides, he was better armed than the Royal Navy men. To save weight, the sloops had not been fitted with cannon, while his own vessel mounted eight big guns. If they wanted to be blown to bits, well, he thought, that was their business.

At sunrise Maynard raised anchor and entered the channel, following carefully behind a rowboat sent ahead to measure the water's depth. In spite of this precaution, both sloops scrunched onto sandbars. Everything that could be spared, including the water barrels, was tossed overboard to lighten the vessels and allow them to float free.

This was Blackbeard's signal to go into action. As the sloops approached, he hoisted the Jolly Roger and shouted across the water: "Damn you for villains, who are you? And from where do you come?"

Lieutenant Maynard ran up the White Ensign of the Royal Navy, a white flag with a red X, and replied: "You may see by our colors we are no pirates."

At this Blackboard became furious. "Damnation seize my soul if I give you quarter or take any from you," he shouted.

"I expect no quarter from you, nor shall I give any," was Maynard's answer. No "quarter" meant no mercy. Only one commander and crew could hope to survive this battle.

The pirates began the battle with a burst of cannon-fire. Blackbeard ordered his chief gunner to train four guns on each sloop, firing them all at once when the enemy came in range.

The effect was terrific: Maynard's escort was ripped from end to end, its commander and most of its crew killed or wounded. Gunfire also raked Maynard's deck, putting twenty-one of his thirty-five crewmen out of action. With a single broadside Blackbeard had cut down his attackers by half.

But Maynard was not the sort of man to give up without a fight. He knew that there was no chance to board the pirate craft in the face of such firepower. The only way to win was to trick Blackbeard into fighting away from the protection of his big guns; that is, to fight aboard his own sloop. Quickly Maynard ordered his men to go below, out of sight, and wait for his signal to come up fighting.

Blackbeard, seeing his enemy badly damaged, moved in for the kill. The ships were only a few yards apart when the pirates let go with a shower of grenades. One after another, like a string of firecrackers, the bottles filled with gunpowder and scrap iron exploded on Maynard's deck. Luckily the deck was empty except for Maynard, his helmsman, and the dead.

"They are all knocked on the head but three or four. Blast you—board her and cut them to pieces!" Blackbeard shouted.

Moments later the ships bumped against one another.

Blackbeard and Lieutenant Maynard duel to the death.

Grappling irons clattered across Maynard's top rail and took hold. Blackbeard was the first to board, followed by ten of his crew.

Maynard's men burst from cover, shouting and shooting as they came. The pirates halted in their tracks, surprised that they still had to fight a battle. They recovered soon enough, though, and the battle became an old-fashioned brawl with cutlasses, knives, and pistols. Kill or be killed. There was no other choice as sweating, panting men fought and skidded across the blood-smeared deck.

Blackbeard waded into the battle, his cutlass whirring. Suddenly he came face to face with Maynard, whose eyes bulged at the first sight of the pirate. Both men fired their pistols pointblank at the same moment. Blackbeard's shot went wild, but Maynard's slammed into his opponent's chest.

Still, an ounce of lead wasn't enough to slow down the big man. He didn't seem to notice that he'd been shot, but kept coming. With one blow of his cutlass he snapped off Maynard's weapon at the hilt. Disarmed, the lieutenant threw the hilt at his enemy. It missed, and he braced for the death blow which he expected any second.

Blackbeard was swinging his cutlass at his enemy's neck when an English sailor came up behind him and slashed him across the neck and throat. He shuddered, missing his swing, which only cut Maynard's knuckles.

Blackbeard's head dangles from the bowsprit of Lieutenant Maynard's vessel as proof that the terrible pirate was, at last, dead.

Howling in pain, he continued to swing his cutlass left and right. But it was no use, for his strength was failing. The English sailors closed in around him, their weapons ready. Again and again, as if he were a cornered beast, they stabbed him from behind or pumped bullets into his chest. At last he pitched forward, landing on his face. He was dead, although it had taken five pistol shots and at least twenty deep stab wounds to kill him.

Seeing their leader killed took away all of his crew's courage. Meekly they dropped their weapons and raised their hands, which were immediately locked in irons. A few days later they paid for their crimes at the end of a rope.

Blackbeard, though, was the true prize. Maynard had the pirate's head cut off and tied to the front of his sloop. With this grizzly trophy swaying to and fro in the breeze, the heroic lieutenant sailed into Bath Harbor.

Legend has it that when Blackbeard's headless body was thrown overboard, it defiantly swam around the sloop a few times before sinking. Whether it did or not doesn't matter anymore. What does matter is that Blackbeard's death marks the end of the "golden age" of piracy.

———◆•◆———

VI

Sisters in Crime:
Women Under the Jolly Roger

November 1720, a courtroom in Port Royal, Jamaica. Dorothy Thomas sits in the witness chair calmly telling of her experiences as a passenger aboard a vessel attacked by pirates. The gunfire and shouting had frightened her, but what really stuck in her mind were two members of the pirate crew. Something about them seemed strange—for pirates. "By the largeness of their breasts," she says, her voice dropping to a whisper, "I believed them to be women."

This *was* strange. The jurors leaned forward to catch her every word. They had never heard such a strange story before. It seemed so fantastic. Everyone knew that seamen didn't like to have women aboard ship. Women were supposed to "jinx" a vessel, to bring it bad luck. Pirates treated female prisoners as cruelly as their menfolk. They held them for ransom, beat them to tell where their valuables were hidden, and mistreated them in other ways. The idea that women might serve aboard a pirate ship as equals, let alone outdo men as fighters, was laughable. Piracy was a for-men-only trade. Men alone had the strength and stamina for battle. Women were soft, gentle creatures who

Mary Read (left) and Anne Bonny proved to be braver than nearly all of the male pirates aboard Captain "Calico Jack" Rackam's ship.

fainted at the cannon's first shot. Everyone knew this, didn't they?

And yet Mistress Thomas's eyes were not playing tricks on her. From time to time women did sail under the Jolly Roger. They did so not as women, but disguised as men.

One of the women Mistress Thomas saw that day was Mary Read. Her story is one of high adventure and, in the end, tragedy. Mary never knew her father, a sailor who disappeared at sea before she was born. Life was harsh, money scarce, in the English country town where Mary and her mother lived. Things became so bad that, when the child turned four, Mrs. Read decided to try a desperate scheme.

Her husband's mother lived in another town, where she had a good income from a small business. Ordinarily, she wouldn't have thought twice about asking her mother-in-law for help. The trouble was that the older woman couldn't stand little girls. Boys she loved, cooing over them and pampering them. Girls made her angry and nasty.

Since she had never seen her grandchild, Mary's mother planned to pass her off as a boy. She spent long hours teaching Mary to act and speak as a boy. Mary's dress was exchanged for a boy's breeches and coat. Dressing as a boy was not as simple as it sounds. Two hundred years ago, wearing the clothes of the opposite sex was a serious matter. Only sinful people, criminals and witches, were thought to disguise themselves in this way.

Mrs. Read's scheme worked beautifully. The grandmother was so impressed with the handsome "lad" that she offered to let the two move in with her. But Mary's mother, seeing the danger of such an arrangement, said they'd rather live in a nearby town. She did, however, accept a weekly allowance which the grandmother offered for their support. This arrangement went on for several years, until the grandmother's death. A teenager by now, Mary decided she would have more opportunities in the world as a man than a woman. And so, at the age of sixteen, or thereabouts, she enlisted in the Royal Navy and was posted to a warship.

It was easier then than now to get away with such a fraud. There were no medical inspections in the 1700s. A young man wishing to join the army or navy simply appeared at the recruiter's office, signed up, and took his first month's pay. That was all. No one asked him to strip or be checked out by a doctor. Servicemen, like everyone else, seldom bathed or washed the entire body. When putting on a uniform, a woman needed only to bind her breasts with a wide sash to pass as a man.

Mary Read, "seaman," soon tired of life in His Majesty's Navy. When her ship next reached port, she deserted and crossed the English Channel to Belgium, where she joined the British Army in the war against France. The life of a Redcoat was as exciting as any adventurer could have wished. Long marches, artillery barrages, bayonet charges: Mary learned war from every angle. She had hoped that bravery would earn her a promotion, but soon learned that poor people couldn't rise through the ranks. An officer's rank was a form of property to be bought and sold to the highest bidder. The richer the person, the higher the rank he was able to purchase.

Disappointed, Mary transferred into a cavalry regiment. One day a new man was put in to share her tent. He was handsome and gentle, and Mary fell in love with him the moment they met. But it was love from the distance, for she was afraid to tell him of her feelings or that his tentmate was a woman.

It took a lot of energy to keep her feelings bottled up; so much that little remained for other things. She became absentminded, neglecting her duties. Surely, the officers thought, Trooper Read was going crazy.

At last Mary blurted out her secret. The young man was amazed, but in time found that he loved her too and asked her to marry him. The officers were so moved by their love story that they decided the wedding should be paid for by the regiment, including the bride's trousseau. For the first time in her life, Mary dressed as a woman, with high-heeled shoes, petticoats, and a low-cut silk dress that made the other soldiers sit up and take notice. The best gift, however, was an honorable discharge for herself and her husband.

Mary's happiness lasted only a few months. She and her husband opened a tavern called "The Three Horseshoes" and were doing well when he died. Brokenhearted, the widow hung up her dress for good and signed on a Dutch merchantman bound for the Caribbean.

Once again Mary Read's life took a sudden turn. Her ship was nearing its destination when it was overtaken by English pirates from New Providence. Not knowing her true identity, only that she spoke English, the pirate captain forced her to join his crew. Mary, who had always loved action and danger, gladly came aboard with her dufflebag.

She saw plenty of action with the pirates, enjoying

every moment of her life at sea. She was so expert with cutlass and pistol, so brave and strong, that the pirates never noticed that their new companion never shaved.

Not that Mary didn't try to "go straight." In 1718, she accepted the king's pardon, settling down in New Providence. It was no good. Life ashore was too quiet, too routine, for one used to the free-roving ways of a pirate. Within a year she packed her gear and shipped out on a privateer.

Of all the privateers cruising the Caribbean, it so happened that there was aboard this one another woman disguised as a man—Mistress Thomas's other pirate. Anne Bonny was the daughter of an Irish lawyer and the family maid. When her father's business failed, he moved to Charleston, South Carolina, where Anne was growing up at the very moment Blackbeard's men came ashore to demand medicines.

Although Anne never met the famous pirate, she had something of his wild temper. Once, when a servant made a mistake, she stabbed her with a carving knife. Yet she must have been attractive, for many fine young men wanted to marry her. She rejected them all in favor of a good-for-nothing sailor named Bonny. Her father was so angry that he threw her out of the house. Penniless, but full of high hopes, the couple set out for New Providence.

They hadn't been at this pirate den long when Anne decided her husband wasn't her type after all. She preferred a flashier sort, like "Calico Jack" Rackam, a conceited dandy if there ever was one. Rackam believed he was God's gift to the world, especially to its women. Dressed in brightly colored calico clothes—hence his nickname—he strutted like a peacock. Mary couldn't take her eyes off him, and before long said good-bye to her husband. There was no divorce; she simply walked out on him.

Calico Jack and his sweetheart, who was disguised as a man to avoid rousing suspicion, were signed aboard the same privateer. After it set sail and New Providence was fading into the distance, Calico Jack and some of his friends mutinied. Anne drew pistols on some loyal crewmen, threatening to blow out their brains if they resisted. Down came the British flag. Up went the Jolly Roger.

Mary and Anne, each thinking the other a man, but knowing themselves to be women, became attracted to each other. Anne especially found herself falling in love with the stranger. Calico Jack, meanwhile, noticed them often together, whispering. Whispering about what? He was becoming jealous of this other "fellow," and was thinking of putting a bullet into him when somehow the women's secret came out. Breathing a sigh of relief, he promised to keep their secret from the crew.

The pirates were having a successful cruise when they ran up alongside of a big merchantman whose captain was a better fighter than most. During the furious battle that followed, most of the ship's crew and several pirates were killed. In order to get back to fighting strength, Calico Jack forced the surviving seamen to sign his articles.

Among the recruits was a softspoken, babyfaced young man. History repeated itself: Mary fell head over heels in love the moment she set eyes on him. This time there was no wasting time. She told him she was a woman and that she loved him. He, for his part, returned her love, promising they would be married at the end of the voyage.

Mary's lover got along well with everyone except one great hulking brute of a pirate. He began to pass remarks and play practical jokes, which the young man didn't think funny. One day he lost his temper and told the pirate what he thought of him. They would have fought then and there, had it not been for the iron rule obeyed on all pirate ships: shipmates could not fight while at sea, for that might cause the crew to take sides, breaking up the entire company. Instead, they made an appointment to fight a duel on a desert island next morning.

Mary was in a panic. Her man was a navigator, not a rough-and-tumble fighter. He knew almost nothing about handling weapons and would be a pushover for his opponent. But *she* was nobody's pushover. Her cutlass was like

"Calico Jack" was a lady's man, but when the chips were down, he ran away and let a woman do his fighting.

an extension of her arm, obeying her every command. The following morning, two hours before the scheduled duel, she walked up to the bully and shouted insults into his face. He turned purple with rage, challenging this big-mouthed "fellow" to a duel then and there. Perfect! He'd walked straight into her trap, she must have thought as they were rowed to the sandy, palm tree-lined beach.

No matter whether it was between noblemen or

pirates, a duel in the 1700s had the formality of a graceful dance. The opponents stood back to back. At the referee's signal, they walked ten paces in either direction,
stopped, and turned to face each other. Each was armed
with double trouble: a pistol and a cutlass.

"Ready," said the referee. They cocked their pistols,
preparing the weapons to fire.

"Aim," the referee called again. Slowly the opponents
raised their right arms, their pistols pointed at each other.
The barrel openings seemed wide, very wide, at ten paces.

"Fire!"

Two shots sounding as one came instantly. The bully
slowly sank to his knees, a wide stain spreading across his
shirt. Mary, unhurt, stepped forward to finish him with
her cutlass. She had saved her darling's life, and he was too
grateful to have any false pride in owing it to a woman.

The career of Calico Jack and his crew came to a sudden end in November 1720. They were cruising near
Jamaica, not expecting trouble, when a coast guard vessel
caught up to them. What followed was more like a game of

*Mary Read finishes off her opponent with her cutlass after the
duel to save her lover's life.*

hide and seek than a battle. Taken by surprise, Calico Jack and his crew panicked and ran belowdecks, hoping to hide in the cargo hold. Only Mary Read, Anne Bonny, and another pirate remained topside to defend the ship.

It was a desperate fight, but one they had to lose. Mary was so angry at her shipmates' cowardice that she raised the hatchcover and shouted for them to come up and fight like men. No one came. Again she raised the hatchcover and fired her pistols, killing one pirate and wounding another. Then the women surrendered.

Their trial in Jamaica was short but not sweet. They had been captured on a ship flying the Jolly Roger and there was no point in wasting words. On November 15, Calico Jack Rackam and his entire crew, including the women, were sentenced to die the next morning. Before they were marched off to Gallows Point, Port Royal, Calico Jack was allowed a last visit with his lover. If he expected her to feel sorry for him, he was mistaken. "I am sorry to see you here, Jack," said Anne, her eyes flashing anger. "But had you fought like a man, you need not have been hanged like a dog."

But the women were not finished yet. Asking to see the judge, they said "My Lord, we plead our bellies." Both were going to be mothers. Execution had to be put off, as English law does not allow hanging a mother-to-be no matter how serious her crimes.

Still, all did not end well for the lady pirates. Mary became ill in jail and died. Whether or not she had her baby, and whether or not it survived, is unknown. Anne disappeared from the prison, and from history, the following year.

———◆◆———

The story of women and piracy doesn't end with Mary and Anne; it only shifts to a different time and part of the world. The time was 1807–1810. The place, the rivers and coasts of China.

Piracy had existed in Asia for thousands of years.

Japanese fleets of over a hundred vessels used to cross the Yellow Sea to China, looting and burning wherever they landed. When word came that the "dwarf people," as the Chinese called the Japanese, were nearby, peasants for hundreds of miles around left the rice paddies and fled with their families to the mountains. They so hated the pirates that captured ones were handed over to specially trained torturers. In some villages captured Japanese pirates were tossed alive into cauldrons of boiling water.

The Chinese also had their native pirates. Skilled sailors, they roamed the rivers and coastal waters in war junks, that is, flat-bottomed boats designed for speed and navigating in shallows. In certain towns, when living space became scarce inside the walls, people moved to junks anchored offshore. Whole families were born, lived, and died without setting foot on land.

China's most feared pirate was a hunchback named Admiral Ching Yih. Born a peasant's son, he was forced to go to sea as a child, for his father couldn't afford to feed him. Life at sea made him hard, and tough, and mean. He turned pirate and, in a few years, gathered around him some of the fiercest captains ever to sail on blue water.

No European sea rover, not even Drake or Morgan, had Admiral Ching Yih's daring and skill in handling large numbers of ships. For this peasant's son commanded not one, but five fleets totaling five hundred war junks and seventy thousand fighting men. Each fleet flew a different color flag and was known by that name: red, yellow, green, black, blue. They were led by officers with poetical names like "Bird and Stone," "Scourge of the Eastern Sea," "Jewel of the Whole Fleet," and "Frog's Meal." The largest fleet, the Red Squadron, was commanded by the admiral's wife, Ching Yih Saou. Everyone, including the admiral, feared this hot-blooded woman.

In 1807, a typhoon, or hurricane at sea, struck the fleets, sinking many junks and drowning Admiral Ching Yih. As was their custom, the Chinese pirates, like their Western brothers, elected a new leader. There was never any doubt who that leader would be. Ching Yih Saou became not only the greatest woman pirate but the greatest pirate of all time. No European admiral commanded so many ships as she; indeed, no navy in Europe or the Americas had as many fighting ships.

Ching Yih Saou ruled her fleet with a hand of iron. Her articles were posted in every vessel for everyone to see. Any seaman who went ashore without permission would have his ears cut off for the first offense; the second offense meant death. Any man who mistreated a woman prisoner was executed. Any man who took loot and failed to put it all in the common treasury was killed as a traitor. No wonder the pirate fleets grew stronger and were more feared than even in her husband's day.

She had to be strict to keep discipline. The emperor of China was pitiless toward any subjects who turned pirate. Hanging was too "mild" a punishment for pirates in old China. They were beheaded and their severed heads stuck on spikes on top of the walls of seaside towns. But punishment didn't stop with the criminal. The pirate's whole family—grandparents, parents, wife, children, uncles, aunts, cousins—were also executed for his crime or sold into slavery.

Life aboard Ching Yih Saou's war junks was cramped, dirty, and uncomfortable. Robert Glasspole, an Englishman captured by the pirates, told of his experiences:

The (pirates) have no settled residence on shore but live constantly in their vessels. The afterpart is reserved for the captain and his wives; he generally has five or six. Every man is allowed a small berth about four feet square, where he stows his wife and family. From the number of souls crowded in so small a space, it must naturally be supposed they are horribly dirty, which is evidently the case, and their vessels swarm with all kinds of vermin: rats in particular they encourage to breed and eat as great delicacies, in fact there are very few creatures they will not eat. During our captivity we lived three weeks on caterpillars boiled with rice!

The Emperor in Peking would have given anything to put Ching Yih Saou out of action. In 1808, he sent Kwo-lang, his best and bravest admiral, after her with a huge fleet. Kwo-lang accepted the mission with many thanks and deep bows. A small man, he had a thin face with a long, wispy goatee beard and mustache. His shiny head was shaved, except for a pigtail that hung down his back to his waist.

The admiral never had a chance. Ching Yih Saou's flagship and a dozen others rode at anchor, seemingly asleep as the imperial fleet bore down on them with banners flying. Admiral Kwo-lang swallowed the bait with a mighty gulp, then it stuck in his throat. For what he couldn't see was the pirate fleets waiting behind a headland, a long strip of land jutting into the sea.

As the Imperial fleet swarmed around Ching Yih Saou's tiny squadron, her fleets attacked from the rear. The battle was fast and furious, with the lady always in the thick of the fighting. She ran about her flagship sprinkling garlic water over the crew to make them bulletproof. It didn't. The Emperor's sailors were amazed to see a woman dressed in red and yellow silks, every one of her shiny black hairs in place, leading an attack with a cutlass.

By sunset, most of Admiral Kwo-lang's ships were sunk, captured, or speeding toward port. The admiral himself was captured and taken aboard Ching Yih Saou's war junk. But the proud man, unable to live with the shame of defeat, committed suicide and died at the feet of the lady pirate.

The Emperor, safe in Peking's Forbidden City, was as determined as ever to destroy the pirates. The "Son of Heaven" had another, stronger, fleet built and sent on its way. He needn't have bothered. As the opposing fleets hove into view, the wind suddenly dropped. They stood motionless, eyeing each other across the water. Ching Yih Saou was not the type to give up just because the wind had died down. She had come for a battle, and a battle she would have. She gave her men such a fiery speech that hundreds leaped overboard, swimming toward the enemy with cutlasses or daggers clamped between their teeth. The Emperor's whole force was captured, together with its admiral.

The Son of Heaven realized at last that if he couldn't defeat his enemy, he'd have to find another, peaceful, way to tame her. Like the European rulers, he offered a pardon, money, and land to any pirate who would settle down.

Success at last! The commander of the Black Squadron surrendered, together with his men and ships. The pirate queen was angry at first, and would have skinned him alive had she been able to capture him. But by 1811, she saw the Emperor's pardon as a chance to enjoy her wealth in peace for the rest of her life. She accepted the pardon and spent her remaining years as head of a large smuggling ring. This wasn't honest work, but the Emperor was satisfied anyhow. For through cunning rather than force, he had done away with the largest pirate fleet of all time.

◆◆

VII

The Barbary Pirates
and the United States Navy

ctober 25, 1793. The Stars and Stripes flutter atop the mainmast of *Polly*, a merchantman out of Boston bound for Cadiz, Spain. She's making good time, speeding ahead of a freshening breeze, when a lookout cries "Sail ho!"

In the distance is another vessel moving swiftly as a racing yacht. Crewmen tense, then relax, when the lookouts report she is flying the British flag. Minutes pass, the stranger gaining by the second, until figures dressed in European clothes can be seen on her deck. Someone calls out in English, asking the American's name and destination. That's when it happens.

The stranger suddenly wisks alongside *Polly*. Grapnels flash across the few yards separating the vessels. Instantly two hundred bearded, turbaned heads rise above the deck rails. Their mouths are open and their shouts can be heard above the rushing sea. Waving pistols and scimitars, the Arab version of the cutlass, the mob leaps aboard *Polly*. The American captain, seeing his men outnumbered five to one, orders the flag hauled down as a signal of surrender. The Barbary pirates have struck again.

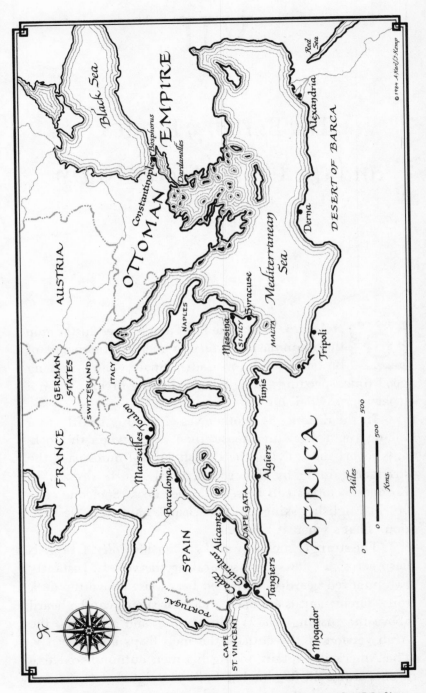

The Barbary Coast and the Countries Bordering the Mediterranean Sea.

The last stronghold of large-scale piracy lay along the two-thousand-mile stretch of North African coast known as the Barbary Coast, so named for the Berber language of its inhabitants. This territory was divided into four Muslim states—Morocco, Algiers, Tunis, Tripoli—that owed allegiance to the Sultan of Turkey. The land is mostly desert, and for centuries the people lived by piracy, although that wasn't what they called it. Their governments demanded "protection money" to allow foreign ships to pass by their coasts in safety. If the money was not paid, or if the foreigners "insulted" them by quibbling over the amount, they declared war. But whatever you called it—war or piracy—sea-roving was big business along the Barbary Coast.

Barbary ships prowled the seas like hungry wolves. The Mediterranean Sea, of course, was their front yard, and most captures were made there. They also ventured onto the Atlantic, braving its storms in search of prey. Between 1569 and 1616, they took 466 ships off the British Isles alone. In 1631, Algerian pirates forced a captured Englishman to write the king: "They say that unless you send money speedily, they will go to England and fetch men out of their beds," which is exactly what they did. Pirates raided seacoast towns and carried hundreds of people into slavery. Pirates even crossed the Atlantic to Iceland, where they burned villages, taking the men, women, and children for sale in Arab slave markets.

Sometimes, when things became really bad, the European powers struck back. Warships bombarded the Barbary Coast, usually without results. The pirate capitals were strongly defended, with high walls and fortresses bristling with cannon. During the French bombardment of Algiers in 1683, the dey (governor) threatened to blow French prisoners from cannon if the attack wasn't called off. He didn't, although several were executed by being tied to chairs in front of the cannon. One Frenchman was stuffed into a wide-mouthed mortar and fired at the fleet. But the Europeans usually gave in without fighting, satisfied to

A French diplomat is loaded into a mortar by Algerians and will be fired at his country's ships standing offshore.

pay millions of dollars for the right to be left alone. Although disgusted at having to bribe such bandits, paying was still cheaper than fighting.

Americans were safe from the Barbary pirates as long as the colonies belonged to Great Britain. The War of Independence changed everything overnight. After the United States became a nation in 1783, its citizens were no longer protected by payments of the mother country; in fact, England encouraged the pirates to attack American shipping as a way of harming a trade rival.

Anxious to avoid trouble, at first the young nation paid protection money. Yet it soon learned that the Barbary pirates, like any blackmailer, could not be bought off for long. They always came back to demand more, more, and more again. They always found excuses to break treaties and capture ships whenever they felt like it.

The capture of *Polly* was only the latest in a long list

of ships taken even though the government paid protection money. Her crew was mistreated from the moment they surrendered. One crewman later wrote:

> . . . the pirates jumped on board us, all armed, some with scimitars and pistols, others with pikes, spears, lances, knives, etc. As soon as they came on board they made signs for us to go forward, assuring us in several languages that if we did not obey their commands they would immediately massacre us all. They then went below into the cabin, steerage and every place where they could get below deck and broke open the trunks and chests there, and plundered all our bedding, clothing, books, charts, quadrants and every movable article. They then came on deck and stripped the clothes off our backs, all except a shirt and a pair of drawers.*

Next day the prisoners were dragged before the dey of Algiers. "Now I have got you, you Christian dogs, you shall eat stones," he said, waving for the guards to take them away. Each man was brought to a blacksmith, who loaded him with forty pounds of chains fastened to the waist and rings clamped around the ankles.

Their prison was a large, overcrowded stone room smelling of garbage and crawling with vermin. Since nothing in Algiers was free, the Americans had to work for their food, a daily ration of one small loaf of black bread dipped in vinegar. All day they toiled under the African sun, hauling rocks to enlarge the harbor. If someone tried to rest, a guard snapped a horsewhip to speed him up. Defending yourself meant death. Rebellious slaves were tossed off the city wall. The lucky ones died instantly, smashed on the rocks below. The unlucky ones were caught on large rusty hooks that jutted from the wall, hanging there for days until death released them from their suffering.

Polly's loss was the last straw. By 1793, Americans realized that only a fleet of warships could protect their

---

* John Foss, *A Journal of the Captivity and Suffering of John Foss*, Newburyport, Massachusetts, 1798.

interests on the high seas. But, a fleet of warships was easier said than done, for the nation had no navy. The Continental Congress had fought the War of Independence at sea with letters of marque and reprisal—1,697 were issued —and a few vessels bought by the government and converted into warships. When the war ended, the privateers were dismissed and the warships sold at auction.

The Barbary pirates proved that even peaceful countries had to be able to defend themselves. On March 27, 1794, Congress passed a bill "To Provide a Naval Armament," which President George Washington signed into law. It was the birth of the United States Navy.

It was a penny-pinching navy, for the young nation couldn't afford the floating fortresses favored by England and France. These battleships, or "ships of the line" as they were called, were many times larger than the galleons of Drake's day. In addition to living quarters and cargo holds, they had three gundecks with upwards of sixty big cannon; each gun could throw a twenty-four- or a thirty-six-pound iron ball nearly a mile. France's *Ville de Paris*, the largest warship in the world, carried one hundred and four cannon.

President Washington decided that the new navy would build frigates, a less powerful type of warship. The frigate had only one gundeck, mounting at most forty-four cannon. Although no *Ville de Paris*, the frigate was still powerful and very fast. The first six ships of the United States Navy were the forty-four-gun *United States*, *President* and *Constitution*, plus the thirty-six-gun *Congress*, *Constellation*, and *Chesapeake*.

Great ships, like anything proud and beautiful, are not built overnight. They are made slowly, carefully, lovingly. These frigates were built by hand by master craftsmen who took pride in their work. Only the best materials were used. The Navy sent out special parties to buy thousands of feet of live oak and cedar, which became hard as iron after months of curing. There was good reason for the USS *Constitution* to be nicknamed "Old Ironsides" during the

"Old Ironside." The frigate USS Constitution *was launched in 1797, first seeing action in the war with the Barbary pirates. She is shown in this old painting with a defeated English ship during the War of 1812.*

War of 1812. British cannon balls just bounced off her hull without doing damage.

Meantime, the United States continued to buy protection and ransom captives, always at escalating prices. Things finally reached a crisis in 1801. The governor of Tripoli became jealous that his rival in Algiers was squeezing more money out of the Yankees than he. Wasn't Tripoli as important as Algiers? Didn't it deserve its "fair share" of American cash? Of course it did! Those stingy sons of Uncle Sam had better pay up, if they knew what was good for them.

No, they wouldn't pay up. Americans, government as well as people, were fed up with the demands of thieving tyrants. Our ambassador was instructed to say that his government expected Tripoli to live up to agreements already signed and paid for.

"No," said the governor in reply. And to underline his point, on May 10, 1801, he had his ruffians chop down the flagpole in front of the American embassy, sending the Stars and Stripes tumbling into the dust. Tripoli had declared war on the United States of America.

The pirate-governor had made the worst mistake of his life. Thomas Jefferson, our third president, had just taken the oath of office and was in no mood to give in to arrogant thugs. Our frigates were ready, and Jefferson sent them to sea with the nation's blessing.

Commanding the squadron was Commodore Richard Dale. The navy of 1801 was too small to have admirals; its highest rank was commodore, the senior captain in charge of a battle group.

Commodore Dale was a good officer, although he lacked the imagination and fighting spirit to cripple the pirates. For two years the Americans blockaded Tripoli with no effect, except to make the pirate captains more cautious when returning to port or putting to sea. Otherwise it was "business as usual" for them.

Then, in July, 1803, news reached the Mediterranean squadron that USS *Constitution* and *Philadelphia* were on their way with a new commander, forty-two-year-old Commodore Edward Preble. No one knew it then, but the Barbary pirates were about to meet their toughest enemy.

Preble was as hard as the granite cliffs of his native Maine. His father, Jedediah Preble, was a retired general who had done well in the shipping business. A great bear of a man, "the Brigadier," as everyone called him, filled the household with laughter at his practical jokes. One day, when Edward was ten, a ship came into Falmouth harbor with a Turkish sailor on board. The Brigadier decided to use this man to see if Edward and his elder brother "had a dash of the right stuff in them." He paid the Turk to act as if he wanted to kidnap the boys. He then went to his sons and told them a fierce Turk was in town looking for little boys to kidnap. He would try to stuff them into a big, smelly sack. When he brought them into his own country, he and his relatives would eat them.

The Preble brothers were sitting alone near the fireplace that night when they heard scratching at the window. In climbed the turbaned Turk, a scimitar at his side and a big sack in his hand. The older boy let out a scream and dived under the bed and out of history. Not Edward. He took a flaming piece of wood from the fireplace and pushed it into the intruder's face, setting his beard ablaze. Yes, indeed, the Brigadier boasted, young Edward had plenty of "the right stuff."

The boy grew into a lonely, silent man, except when his temper flared. Then junior officers wished they'd never heard of the United States Navy. Discipline aboard Preble's ships was as unbending as a steel rod, and the Lord have mercy upon anyone who wasn't as perfect as the commodore expected him to be. Edward Preble, in short, was an easy person to hate.

The crews shuddered when he took charge of the Mediterranean squadron. "They have given me nothing but a pack of boys!" he said with a snort when the junior officers turned out for inspection. They *were* a pack of boys, these lieutenants of 1803. All were in their early twenties, yet, he'd find, they also had "the right stuff." Among them were Isaac Hull and Stephen Decatur, who would become heroes in the War of 1812.

The young men soon learned to admire one thing about their commodore: he was the fightingest naval officer the United States had produced since John Paul Jones. One night, as *Constitution* was passing through the Straits of Gibraltar, a large man-of-war suddenly came crashing out of the darkness. Preble called out his ship's name, but the

The Barbary Pirates and the United States Navy 149

captain of the other vessel remained silent. Again and again Preble asked the stranger to identify himself. Silence.

"I now hail you for the last time," Preble called, "if you do not answer I'll fire a shot into you."

"If you do, I'll return a broadside," came the reply in perfect English.

"I should like to catch you at that! I now hail you for an answer. What ship is that?"

"This is His Britannic Majesty's eighty-four-gun ship of the line *Donegal*. Send a boat aboard." The Englishman wanted the American to prove his identity by sending a rowboat with an officer with his ship's papers.

Preble, his face flushed with anger, barked: "This is the United States forty-four-gun ship *Constitution*, Captain Edward Preble, and I'll be damned if I send a boat on board any ship! Blow on your matches, boys!"

The American gunners stood over their weapons with smoking matches, ready to fire a broadside. It wasn't necessary, for the English captain backed down; *he* sent a boat to identify himself. The "boys" looked at one another and winked, broad smiles crossing their faces. Old pickleface was a tough customer.

While Commodore Preble set up his headquarters at Syracuse on the island of Sicily, USS *Philadelphia*, with thirty-five-guns, under Captain William Bainbridge, went on blockade station off Tripoli. A gift to the Navy from the city for which she was named, *Philadelphia* was as unlucky as she was beautiful.

On the morning of October 31, 1803, *Philadelphia*'s lookouts sighted a Tripolitan vessel making for port under full sail. Captain Bainbridge sent his sailors scuttling up the shrouds to tack on every inch of canvas the masts could carry.

Philadelphia took off after the Tripolitan. She could have caught her in the open sea, for she was built for speed and easy handling. But the approaches to Tripoli harbor are dangerous. Long reefs broken by shallow channels guard the entrance. The Tripolitan captain knew the channels like the back of his hand. Bainbridge didn't.

The Tripolitan was scooting around the reefs, *Philadelphia* close behind, when the American vessel ran aground. A harsh scraping noise was followed by a sudden jolt, which knocked crewmen off their feet, sending them tumbling across the deck. *Philadelphia*'s bow rose six feet out of the water as she became stuck on a submerged rock ledge.

Bainbridge tried everything to lighten the bow in the hope that *Philadelphia* would slip off her perch. The foremast was cut away. Anchors were cut loose. Cannon and supplies went overboard. The ship moved, tilting to the port (left) side, which made it impossible to aim the remaining cannon.

The Tripolitans, seeing the American warship in trouble, sent out their own fighting vessels. Tripolitan gunboats swarmed around *Philadelphia*, pouring cannon balls into her. She was defenseless. To avoid a massacre, Bainbridge decided to surrender. But before giving up the ship, he tried to make her useless to the enemy. Her magazine was flooded and the remaining guns rolled overboard. Her pumps were blocked and holes drilled through her bottom. Then the captain and three hundred and fourteen officers and men surrendered.

Preble was stunned when he learned of *Philadelphia*'s loss. Losing her was bad enough, but what really worried him was news that waves had shaken her off the reef. The pirates then unstuffed her pumps, plugged the holes in her bottom, salvaged her cannon from the shallows, and towed her into Tripoli harbor to be refitted as a pirate vessel. Once she became seaworthy again, the pirates would have a warship as powerful as anything in the American squadron. The Americans had no choice but to destroy her with their own hands.

The man chosen for this job was twenty-five-year-old Lieutenant Stephen Decatur, Jr., skipper of the support ship

USS *Enterprise*, twelve guns. Decatur's mother had wanted him to be a bishop; he was a sickly child, and she thought a life free from excitement would restore his health. Stephen senior, a privateer captain, had other ideas. He took the youngster on a long cruise during which, it seems, the smell of salt air cured his illness.

Decatur was a Yankee fire-eater. Handsome and hot-tempered, he never ran away from trouble. And trouble always had a way of finding him. He once had himself rowed ashore at the Spanish port of Barcelona to buy supplies. His longboat flew the Stars and Stripes. Yet, as it passed a Spanish warship, the captain fired a cannon shot across his path. He wanted the American to come aboard to identify himself. Decatur kept going; on the way back the warship let him have another shot.

Next morning Decatur, in full uniform, came aboard the Spanish warship and asked to see the captain. Luckily —for the captain—he was ashore. "Very well," said Decatur loud enough for everyone to hear, "you may tell him that Lieutenant Decatur pronounces him a cowardly scoundrel, and when they meet on shore will cut his ears off." The Spaniard made sure they never met. Decatur's men spoke of his courage, and how they would follow him anywhere.

Now they had their chance. Decatur gathered his men and told them of the dangers that lay ahead. *Philadelphia* was in Tripoli harbor, at the center of the pirates' defense system. Between her and the shore were anchored nineteen gunboats. Towering above her, a stone's throw away, was the governor's castle with one hundred and fifteen heavy cannon peering from gun ports. Ashore, manning other batteries, were twenty-five thousand troops.

Decatur's plan was simple—and dangerous. *Enterprise* had recently captured a Tripolitan ship, which was re-named the *Intrepid*.* She would carry a boarding party to

---

* United States Navy aircraft carriers are named for famous ships and battles. Some of the most famous carriers of World War II took their names from ships that served in Preble's squadron: *Enterprise, Essex, Intrepid.*

Stephen Decatur lead the daring night raid to destroy the USS Philadelphia, *which had fallen into the hands of the pirates of* Tripoli.

Philadelphia that would blow her sky-high before the pirates knew what was happening.

Any volunteers? Every man and boy aboard *Enterprise* stepped forward. Sixty-eight of her officers and men, plus six officers from *Constitution*, were selected for the mission. Salvadore Catalano, a Sicilian navigator familiar

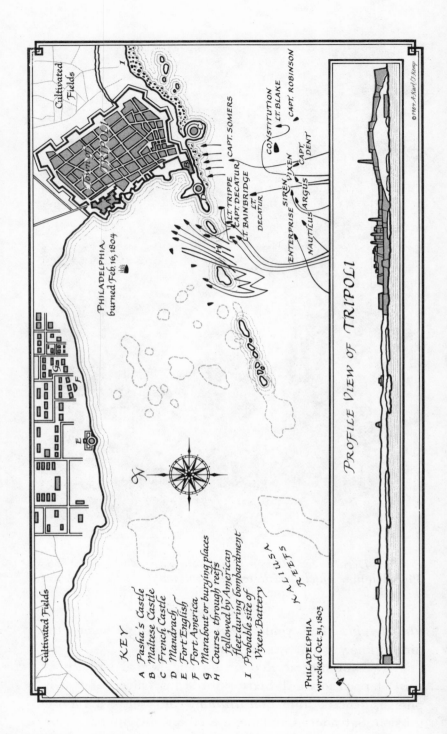

Cultivated Fields

Town of TRIPOLI

Cultivated Fields

PHILADELPHIA burned Feb.16, 1804

PHILADELPHIA wrecked Oct. 31, 1803

KALIUSA REEFS

CONSTITUTION
LT. BLAKE

CAPT. ROBINSON

CAPT. SOMERS
LT. TRIPPE
CAPT. DECATUR
LT. BAINBRIDGE
LT. DECATUR

VIXEN
CAPT. DENT

SIREN
ARGUS
NAUTILUS
ENTERPRISE

PROFILE VIEW OF TRIPOLI

© 1984 · A Karl / J Kemp

KEY

A Pasha's Castle
B Maltese Castle
C French Castle
D Mandrach
E Fort English
F Fort America
G Marabout or burying places
H Course through reefs
    followed by American
    fleet during bombardment
I Probable site of
    Vixen Battery

---

with Tripoli harbor, went along to guide them through the reefs.

On the night of February 16, 1804, tiny *Intrepid* set out under a full moon. The city's lights burned brightly behind the darkened batteries along the shore. There was no turning back.

At ten o'clock the *Philadelphia* came into view across the harbor. Her lanterns were lit. Light streamed through her open portholes like so many searching eyes. Decatur ordered his men to lie flat on deck or hide in darkened corners. Only he, Catalano, and a few others dressed as Arabs showed themselves.

Closer, closer they came until a guard challenged them from the frigate. The Americans sucked in their breath, tightening their grip on their weapons. Catalano explained that he wanted to tie up alongside the frigate for the night, because his ship had lost its anchors and he didn't want to blunder about in the darkness. The pirate captain believed his story and ordered someone to toss out a line. The pirates bent their backs, pulling *Intrepid* toward them.

As she bumped against *Philadelphia*'s side, a deck-hand looked down. There, in plain view, were the anchors. And there, crouching on deck, were—"Amerikano! Amerikano!"

"*Board!*" shouted Decatur as he sprang onto *Philadelphia*'s deck. His comrades followed, swarming over the rails and through the open gunports. Twenty pirates were cut down in the first fury of the American attack. From the bow Decatur could hear the quick splash, splash, splashing of the others diving overboard.

Decatur's men had no time to admire their handiwork. Any moment and the enemy would discover what they were up to and counterattack. Small groups ran through

The burning of the Philadelphia *in Tripoli harbor, February 16, 1804.*

---

the ship, placing gunpowder and kerosene in key spots. Then someone threw a torch.

Philadelphia was a roaring inferno when the boarders returned to their ship and cast off. Decatur, the first to board, was also the last to leave. *Intrepid* was swinging clear when he made a running jump into her shrouds.

The Americans sailed for dear life. They were a perfect target in the moonlight and the glare of the burning vessel. Fountains of water tossed up by cannonballs rose around *Intrepid.* Luckily the enemy gunners were too excited to aim carefully, and only one shot passed through a sail. Equally dangerous were *Philadelphia's* own guns, which had been loaded with two cannonballs apiece. These guns went off as the fire reached them, spraying cannonballs at the fleeing Americans.

Decatur's men were too amazed by the sight to be scared. Never did a proud ship meet her end with such dignity and, to tell the truth, with such beauty. *Philadelphia's* fires lit up the harbor, throwing banners of orange flame in every direction. The whole vessel—hull, masts, deck—was outlined in fire against the night sky. Her shrouds burned, resembling an enormous spider's web. Black tar melted in the terrific heat, boiled, and ran down her sides in great globs.

Hearing the commotion, the people of Tripoli ran to the housetops to see what was the matter. They couldn't believe their eyes. *Philadelphia* had broken loose from her cables and drifted under the walls of the governor's castle, exploding with an earthshaking roar. Flaming timbers flew skyward, tracing graceful curves of light as they drifted down. Then silence, except for the hissing of ship's wreckage as it smoldered through the night. Now the pirates could keep *Philadelphia.*

Decatur—*Captain* Stephen Decatur, USN—was the hero of the hour. England's Admiral Lord Horatio Nelson, himself no stranger to daring deeds, called the exploit "the most bold and daring act of the age." Pirate-haters the world over smiled and put the young American's name down in their books as a good man to watch.

◆·◆

Commodore Preble didn't smile. It was all well and good to burn *Philadelphia*, but he knew wars aren't won by burning your own ships. Wars are won by putting the enemy out of action.

This is exactly what Preble now set out to do. After spending several months making preparations, Preble returned to Tripoli in the summer of 1804. He came with

*Michele F. Corne's painting shows Commodore Preble's squad-
ron bombarding the port of Tripoli in August 1804.*

nearly eleven hundred men and one hundred and thirty-
four cannon. Opposing him were twenty-five thousand
Tripolitan soldiers and two hundred cannon. Preble
thought the odds to be about "even."

The Commodore's plan was not to capture Tripoli,
but to clamp a tight blockade on the port. No ship, regardless of its country, would be allowed to enter or leave.
Using the mobile firepower of his frigates, he intended to
tear up the shore defenses and destroy any pirate vessel
caught in the harbor.

The Americans' first attack, August 3, 1804, handed
the pirates the worst defeat they had ever suffered. Preble's
fleet sailed into the harbor in line-ahead formation, one
ship behind the other, challenging the pirate ships to a
slugging match. The Tripolitans came out, but not to trade

broadsides. Although poor at long-range gunnery, they prided themselves at hand-to-hand fighting. No one had been able to match them at this skill in over three hundred years—no one until this morning.

As the frigates pounded Tripoli, the pirate craft rushed a portion of the supporting squadron under Decatur. The battle quickly became a ship-against-ship free-for-all. Decatur pulled up alongside the nearest enemy vessel and, as usual, was the first to leap aboard. His men followed with pistols, pikes, cutlasses, and Indian tomahawks. After a short time two pirate ships had been captured by Decatur and a fellow officer.

Meanwhile his younger brother, James Decatur, a lieutenant, had tangled with another pirate vessel. At the right moment he let loose a broadside of guns charged with grapeshot, canvas bags filled with hundreds of musket balls apiece. His first volley did such damage that the pirate captain hauled down his flag as a sign of surrender. Yet it was only a trick. For as young Decatur climbed aboard to claim his prize, the pirate shot him with a pistol then made a dash for safety.

He never made it. News of his brother's death was brought to Decatur as he was towing away his own prize. Shouting for his unwounded men to join him—only eleven were still in shape to fight—he cut the prize loose and sped after the treacherous pirate. One of these men had to die.

Decatur didn't bother to slow down when he caught up to enemy. He just slammed into him at top speed and jumped aboard. The pirate captain was a tall, muscular man with the strength of a wrestler and the cunning of a streetfighter. He raised his spear the instant Decatur swung his cutlass at his head. CRAACK! The cutlass blade snapped off at the hilt. Down came the spearpoint, carving a red channel across Decatur's arm and chest.

Ignoring his wounds, Decatur jumped on his opponent, dragging him down. Seeing them, one man after another piled on top, each trying to help his own captain.

The mass of desperate men grappled on the rolling deck, each trying to kill the other.

The pirate captain had one hand around Decatur's throat, squeezing with all his might. With the other hand he fumbled for a dagger in his belt. Decatur tried to break his hold while groping for a small pistol in his pocket. Out it came, when suddenly he saw looming over him a pirate with a scimitar. He was swinging it when an American sailor named Reuben James deliberately stood in the way. James took a nasty cut on his head but survived. Decatur fired, killing the pirate captain instantly. That did it. The other pirates surrendered or dived overboard. Never again would the Barbary pirates challenge United States Navy men to a fight at close quarters.

Decatur's biggest surprise came when he climbed aboard *Constitution* to report his victories to Preble. Pale from grief and loss of blood, his uniform torn to shreds, he said, "I have brought you three of the enemy's gunboats, sir."

The Commodore, his lips squeezed tight, grabbed Decatur by the collar and shook him so his teeth rattled. "Aye, sir!" he shouted into his face. "And why did you not bring me more?" Then he turned on his heel and went to his cabin.

"The commodore wishes to see Captain Decatur in his cabin, sir," said another officer.

Decatur went below, into the captain's cabin shaking with anger at Preble's insult. For a long time—it felt like hours to the crew—not a sound came from behind the closed door. What was wrong? Could they have killed each other? Finally an officer tapped on the door and flung it open. Commodore and captain were seated side by side on a narrow wooden bench, tears rolling down their cheeks. Neither man ever told what happened during their meeting. All we know is that no one in the early 1800s thought it wrong for strong men to let out their feelings by crying.

The American squadron now began to bombard Tripoli regularly. *Constitution* and her sister ships sailed up to the defenses and cut loose with their big guns at pointblank range. Specially built ships rented from the king of Sicily lobbed kettle-sized bombs into the city.

Preble was squeezing the life out of Tripoli when word came that he was being replaced by Commodore Samuel Barron, a senior officer. Old pickle-face had to leave, but what a send-off they gave him! With Decatur leading, the officers lined up to shake his hand and thank him for being their commander. Under him they had become experienced combat officers. And from that day on, they were proud to be called "Preble's boys."

Commodore Barron finished the work Preble had begun. By the spring of 1805, Tripoli was ready to make peace. The Americans agreed to pay sixty thousand dollars for *Philadelphia*'s crew in exchange for an end to "protection" payments. Never again, Tripoli's governor promised, would his pirates molest American ships.

———◆•◆———

Ten years would pass before the United States finished its business with the Barbary pirates. Growing troubles with England meant that every fighting ship was needed to guard our coasts. The pirate states breathed a sigh of relief and waited for an excuse to teach those stubborn Yankees a lesson.

The War of 1812 gave them their chance. The British ambassador told Governor Hadji Ali of Algiers that "the American flag will be swept from the seas, the contemptible navy of the United States annihilated and its marine arsenals reduced to a heap of ruins." The Royal Navy was the largest in the world, having a thousand warships mounting twenty-eight thousand cannon; the United States Navy had only seventeen first-class ships mounting fewer than four hundred and fifty guns. Hadji Ali liked a winner, and England certainly seemed like a winner. He declared war on the United States and sent his admiral, Rais Hammida, "the terror of the Mediterranean," to sweep the sea clear of American ships.

He should have kept his mouth shut and sat on his hands. His English allies let him down at every turn. Not that they wanted to; they couldn't help themselves. Preble's boys, now captains and commodores, shot the Royal Navy's proudest ships to pieces. Decatur captured *Macedonian*; Isaac Hull sank *Guerrière*. James Lawrence was killed in action, but his dying words, "Don't give up the ship!" have become a motto of the Navy.

The ink was hardly dry on the peace treaty of 1815 when President James Madison sent two powerful squadrons to the Mediterranean to deal with the Barbary pirates once and for all. Decatur sailed with the USS *Guerrière*, named after the British man of war; *Macedonian*, now proudly flying the American flag; *Constitution* ("Old Ironsides"); and several smaller vessels. William Bainbridge followed with *United States*, *Congress*, and *Independence*, a spanking-new seventy-four-gun ship of the line. Bainbridge might as well have stayed home, for Decatur had finished the war by the time he arrived on station.

Decatur's squadron had just passed the Straits of Gibraltar, June 17, when lookouts saw an Algerian vessel. She was the frigate *Mashuda*, pride of the Algerian fleet, commanded by none other than Rais Hammida. The pirate admiral sped for the Spanish coast and neutral waters when he saw his danger.

He never made it. *Guerrière*, the wind billowing her sails, her sleek hull knifing through the water, overtook *Mashuda* without any trouble. Rais Hammida turned, unleashing broadsides one after another at the oncoming American. Decatur ignored the fountains of water that shot up in *Guerrière*'s path and the sharp splinters whirling through the air. He urged his men on, until the ships' yardarms were almost touching.

"Fire!" he shouted through a brass speaking trumpet.

Guerrière's veteran gunners gave the Algerians a steady twenty-five-minute "salute" of iron and fire. Grape-

shot mowed down the crew, turning *Mashuda*'s deck slippery with blood. Cannon balls—forty-two-pounders—
punched holes in her sides. One ball caught Rais Hammida,
cutting him in half. The survivors surrendered.

Decatur now raced across the Mediterranean for Algiers, blasting every pirate ship he met along the way. On

A watercolor painting of the Enterprise *in 1820, firing on pirate vessels when she took part in the final sweep to destroy piracy in the Caribbean.*

June 29, the Americans burst into Algiers harbor, the Stars and Stripes snapping atop each ship's mainmast. Gunners stood at their posts with matches lit and ready for action. It was the pirates' moment of truth.

Decatur had not come to pay ransom, or protection money, or to bargain. There was nothing to discuss. He had come to give the pirate state America's terms or to fight. And these terms were stiff: no more capturing American ships; prisoners to be released without ransom; owners of captured ships to be paid for their troubles. Take it or leave it!

The governor's messenger was shocked. No one had ever spoken to Algerians with such disrespect. The messenger asked for a three-hour truce to allow his master to think over the terms.

"Not a minute!" snapped Decatur. Either the Algerians accepted his terms or he'd open fire. The messenger scurried away, mumbling about crazy young sea captains in blue. An hour later the governor's personal barge came out under a flag of truce. On board was the signed treaty and a group of American prisoners. Some broke down, crying for joy as they kissed the Stars and Stripes.

The rest of the voyage was more like a victory parade than a military campaign. Tunis and Morocco fell into line the moment they stared down the barrels of Decatur's cannon. These spoke a language any dictator could understand. Tripoli, which had been thinking of breaking the treaty of 1805, had second thoughts. Instead, it gave a thirty-one-gun salute to the Stars and Stripes as Decatur's squadron glided past the governor's castle.

America's Barbary Wars were over. They had been fought for national honor and a principle. As Decatur's squadron sailed for the Straits of Gibraltar and home, it met seven Algerian warships in battle formation. What did they want? Decatur didn't know, but he cleared for action.

When the Algerians came within calling distance, their admiral cried, *"Dove andante?"* (Where are you going?) Decatur's voice rang across the water, loudly, defiantly, proudly: *"Dove mi piace!* (Where it pleases me.)

And so it was, and so it always has been since then. American ships sail where they please.

———— ◆•◆ ————

The victories of Preble and his boys signaled the end of sea roving as a menace to the world's trade. In the years that followed, the maritime nations joined forces to stamp out piracy. The United States Navy and the Royal Navy cooperated in the 1820s to destroy the remains of piracy in the Caribbean. France conquered Algeria in 1830, crippling the pirate states forever. The Declaration of Paris, 1856, outlawed privateering, for centuries the main source of manpower for pirate ships.

Never again would Drakes and Morgans and Kidds and their bloody kin menace the world's trade. The seas, like the skies, remain open for all peoples to enjoy in peace.

———— ◆•◆ ————

Some More Books

Allen, George W. *Our Navy and the Barbary Corsairs*. Hamden,
    Conn.: Archon Books, 1905.
Carse, Robert. *The Age of Piracy*. New York: Rinehart & Co.,
    1957.
Chidsey, Donald B. *The Wars in Barbary: Arab Piracy and the
    Birth of the United States Navy*. New York: Crown Pub-
    lishers, 1971.
Cochran, Hamilton. *Freebooters of the Red Sea*. Indianapolis:
    Bobbs-Merrill, Inc., 1965.
Gosse, Philip. *The History of Piracy*. New York: Burt Franklin,
    1968.
————. *The Pirates' Who's Who*. New York: Burt Franklin,
    1968.
Jobé, Joseph, editor. *The Great Age of Sail*. New York: New
    York Graphic Society, 1967.
Johnson, Captain Charles (Daniel Defoe). *A General History of
    the Robberies and Murders of the Most Notorious Pirates*,
    London, 1724; reprinted, London: Routledge & Kegan
    Paul, 1926.
Kemp, Peter. *The British Sailor*. London: J.M. Dent, 1970.
Lee, Robert E. *Blackbeard the Pirate*. Winston-Salem, N.C.:
    John F. Blair, 1974.
Means, P.A. *The Spanish Main*. New York: Scribners, 1935.
Morison, Samuel Eliot. *The European Discovery of America:
    The Southern Voyages, 1492–1616*. New York: Oxford
    University Press, 1969.

Pratt, Fletcher. *Preble's Boys: Commodore Preble and the Birth of American Sea Power*. New York: William Sloane, 1950.

Pringle, Patrick. *Jolly Roger: The Story of the Great Age of Piracy*. New York: W.W. Norton, 1953.

Rankin, Hugh R. *The Golden Age of Piracy*. New York: Holt, Rinehart and Winston, Inc., 1969.

Roberts, W. Adolphe. *Sir Henry Morgan*. New York: Covici & Friede, 1933.

Snow, Edward R. *Pirates and Buccaneers of the Atlantic Coast*. Boston: Yankee Publishing Co., 1944.

Sternbeck, Alfred. *Filibusters, Buccaneers, and Pirates*. New York: Robert M. McBride, no date.

Unwin, Rayner. *The Defeat of John Hawkins: A Biography of His Third Slaving Voyage*. New York: Macmillan, 1960.

Williams, Neville. *Captains Outrageous: Seven Centuries of Piracy*. New York: Macmillan, 1962.

Wilson, Derek, *The World Encompassed: Francis Drake and His Great Voyage*. New York: Harper & Row, 1977.

Woodbury, George. *The Great Days of Piracy in the West Indies*. New York: W.W. Norton, 1951.

Index

Ali, Hadji, 162
Anton, Juan de, 29, 30
Avery, Henry ("Long Ben"),
    101–105

Bainbridge, Captain William,
    150, 151
Barbary pirates
    early history, 141–144; wars
    with United States, 148–
    167
Barron, Commodore Samuel,
    162
Bartholomeo the Portuguese,
    56–57
Bellomont, Earl of, 101, 114
Blackbeard, 118–127, 132
Bonny, Anne, 132–136
British East India Company,
    92, 105, 114
brothers of the coast
    see buccaneers
buccaneers
    origins, life, methods of
    attack, 39–55

Caesar, Julius, ix
Campo, Don Alonso de, 74, 76
Castellon, Governor of Porto
    Bello, 60–71
Castelano, Salvadore, 153–155
Charles II, King, 86
Cimarrons, 20–24, 80
Columbus, Christopher, x, 8
Cortlandt, Stephanus van, 89
Culliford, Captain, 113

Dale, Commodore Richard, 148
Decatur, James 160
Decatur, Stephen, 149, 151–
    158, 160–167
Declaration of Paris, 164
Defoe, Daniel, 119
Delancey, Stephen, 89
Diego, escaped Negro slave,
    20, 24
Doughty, Thomas, 25, 26
Drake, Edmund, 45
Drake, Francis, 45, 66, 80, 137,
    146; early life and
    voyages, 3–4; slaving

Drake (continued)
   voyage to the New World,
     5–14; captures Spanish
     treasure on the Isthmus
     of Panama, 14–24;
     circumnavigates the globe,
     24–32; knighted, 33;
     death, 33
Drake, John, 15, 18, 20, 21
Drake, Joseph, 15

Eden, Charles, 122
Elizabeth I, Queen, 5, 6, 10,
   16, 24, 32–33
Enriquez, Don Martin, 10, 11,
   12
Esquemeling, John, 56, 58, 80,
   81

Fletcher, Benjamin, 89, 95, 109

Glasspole, Robert, 138
Great Mogul of India, 91–92,
   114

Hammida, Rais, 163, 164
Hawkins, John, 5, 8–14, 34, 45
Hornigold, Benjamin, 118
Hull, Captain Isaac, 149, 163

James, Reuben, 161
Jefferson, President Thomas,
   148
Jones, John Paul, 149

Kidd, Captain William
   early life, 108–109; turns
     pirate, 110–114; arrested
     and executed, 114–118
Kwo-lang, Admiral, 137

L'Olonnois, 57–58, 71, 72
Lawrence, James, 163
Le Grand, Pierre, 44–45
letters of marque and
   reprisal, 61

Madison, President James, 163
Magellan, Ferdinand, 26
Mansveldt, Edward, 64
Maynard, Lieutenant Robert,
   123–127
Modyford, Sir Thomas, 64–65,
   85
Montbars the Exterminator,
   56
Morgan, Henry
   early life, 59–61; arrives in
     Jamaica, 61–64; rise to
     power, 64–65; captures
     Porto Bello, Panama, 66–
     71; captures Maracaibo,
     Venezuela, 71–73;
     captures Gibraltar,
     Venezuela, 73–78;
     captures Panama City, 78–
     85; knighted and dies, 86
Morgan, Robert, 60

Nau, Jean-David
   see L'Olonnois
Navigation Acts, 88
Nelson, Lord Horatio, 158
Nombre de Dios, Panama,
   15, 16–20, 23, 66

Ocracoke Island, 123–127

Panama City, 15, 22, 23, 78–85
Pearl Islands, 15
Penn, Admiral William, 61
Philip II, King, 9, 16, 24, 33, 34
Philipse, Frederick, 89
Phillips, Captain John, 89

Piracy
  beginnings in the New
    World, 87–91; spreads to
    Red Sea, 91–93; bases on
    Madagascar, 95–97;
    flags, 97–100; methods of
    attacks, 98–101; women
    pirates, 128–140
Port Royal, Jamaica, 59, 62–63
Preble, Commodore Edward,
  148–150, 158–159, 161–
  162, 167
Preble, Jedediah, 148

Rackham, "Calico Jack," 132–
  136
Reed, Mary, 129–136

San Juan de Ulua, Mexico,
  9–14, 18
Saou, Ching Yih, 137–140
Ships
  Adventure Galley, 110, 112,
    113, 114
  Amity, 93
  Angel, 6
  Benedict, 25, 26
  Chesapeake, USS, 146
  Congress, USS, 146, 163
  Constellation, USS, 146
  Constitution, USS (Old
    Ironsides"), 146, 148,
    149, 153, 161, 162, 163
  Donegal, HMS, 150
  Duke, 101
  Elizabeth, 25, 27
  Enterprise, USS, 152
  Essex, USS, 152
  Golden Hind, 25, 27, 29, 30,
    32, 34
  Guerriere, HMS, 163
  Gunsway, 103
  Intrepid, USS, 152, 157
  Jesus, 8, 9, 10, 12, 13, 16
  Judith, 6, 7, 14
  Lyme, HMS, 123
  Magdalena, 76
  Macedonian, HMS, 163
  Marigold, 25, 27
  Mashuda, 164
  Minion, 12, 14
  *Nuestra Señora de la
    Concepcion (Cacafuego)*,
    28–29, 31–32
  Oxford, 71
  Pasha, 15
  Pearl, HMS, 123
  Philadelphia, USS, 148,
    150–158, 162
  Polly, 141, 144, 145
  President, USS, 146
  Quedah Merchant, 113
  Queen Anne's Revenge, 118
  Swallow, 6
  Swan, 25, 26
  United States, USS, 146, 163
  Ville de Paris, 146
  William and John, 6
Slave Coast, Africa, 6–7
Spotswood, Alexander, 122–123
Straits of Magellan, 25, 26, 27

Teach, Edward
  see Blackbeard
Tetu, Captain, 23
Tew, Thomas, 92–95, 101, 109
Thomas, Dorothy, 128–129
Tortuga Island, 43–45
Trott, Nicholas, 103–104

United States Navy
  creation and early vessels,
    146

Vikings, ix

Washington, President George,
  146
William III, King, 111, 114

Yih, Admiral Ching, 137